MAID FOR
THE UNTAMED
BILLIONAIRE

MAID FOR THE UNTAMED BILLIONAIRE

MIRANDA LEE

MILLS & BOON

First published in Great Britain 2019
by Mills & Boon, an imprint of HarperCollins*Publishers*
1 London Bridge Street, London, SE1 9GF

Large Print edition 2020

© 2019 Miranda Lee

ISBN: 978-0-263-08918-9

MIX
Paper from
responsible sources
FSC C007454

This book is produced from independently certified
FSC™ paper to ensure responsible forest management. For
more information visit www.harpercollins.co.uk/green.

Printed and bound in Great Britain
by CPI Group (UK) Ltd, Croydon, CR0 4YY

Dedicated to my sister, Wendy.
A lovely lady and my best friend.

PROLOGUE

JAKE NEEDED A HOUSEKEEPER.

But not the live-in kind. The last thing he wanted was someone underfoot all the time, picking up after him, forcing him to make conversation and invading his space. The reason Jake had bought a house a few years ago was to have his own space.

After spending weeks in hospital and then another month at the rehabilitation clinic, he'd wanted nothing more than to be by himself. So he'd turned down the offers to live with relatives and bought this place in East Balmain, calling it a thirtieth birthday present to himself.

He'd thought he could make do with a cleaner coming in three times a week. And he *had* managed—in a fashion, even in the beginning when he'd been pretty useless, his leg still not totally healed. He'd shopped online and sent his laundry out, a routine he'd continued even after he was fully better and back working.

But it had finally become tedious, seeing to all the other chores which owning and maintaining a house involved. He loathed having to wait for tradespeople, who didn't always turn up on time. Patience was not his strong suit.

Jake could well afford to pay someone to do everything for him. He'd already been a wealthy man before the success of his television show, so it had never been a matter of money. More of privacy.

Not that he had much privacy any more, his star having risen over the last couple of years, his every move recorded on social media and in the gossip rags.

But not at home. His home was his sanctuary, as well as his castle. So it was imperative that Jake find the right kind of housekeeper, a task which had proven to be much more difficult than he'd assumed, mostly because he simply hadn't *liked* any of the women he'd interviewed for the position.

It was silly, really, given he wouldn't have to have anything much to do with the woman on a personal basis. His brief to the various employment agencies was for his housekeeper to work only during the week, not at the weekends. She was to come in after he left for work every weekday morning, and be gone by the time he arrived home, which often wasn't until quite late. Producing and hosting *Australia at Noon* consumed every minute of every weekday from morning until late afternoon.

So it shouldn't really matter whether he liked his housekeeper or not.

But he couldn't stomach the thought of someone he didn't like in his personal space when he wasn't there.

The main problem was that every woman he'd interviewed so far had been a big fan of his show. Not a crime, admittedly. But irritating. They had all been way too gushy. And way too eager.

Jake was suspicious of eager, especially when it came to women. A flaw, he supposed, common with confirmed bachelors. Still, he kept picturing them putting things about their *wonderful* new job and their *wonderful* new boss on all the social media sites they would invariably be on, complete with photos.

The upshot was he hadn't hired any of them, and was instead waiting for another candidate to arrive, sent out by Housewives For Hire, a newish employment agency, the owner of which had fortuitously appeared on a segment of his show a few days ago.

Her agency promised to provide exactly the sort of employee he was looking for. Apparently, the women on their books were mostly housewives themselves, wanting to earn extra money whilst their children were at school.

He'd rung the lady who owned the agency the other night—her name was Barbara—explaining what kind of housekeeper he needed. He'd asked her to find him someone suitable, preferably a woman who didn't obsessively watch his show and think he was God's gift to women.

She'd promised to find him the right person.

So here he was, sitting in his study at five to two on a Saturday afternoon, waiting to interview Barbara's top recommendation, but thinking to himself he was possibly wasting his time again.

This woman Barbara was sending him was way too young for starters. Only twenty-six. And a widow no less. How on earth had that happened?

Barbara hadn't said and he hadn't liked to ask.

Jake sighed. A car accident, he supposed. Or an illness of some kind.

At least she didn't have children. Nothing sadder than a young widow trying to raise children alone. Nothing tougher, either.

This young woman—her name was Abby Jenkins—was apparently looking for work and wasn't qualified for much, her very short CV showing she had left high school at seventeen to work in a fish and chip shop till she'd married at twenty, shortly after which she'd left to become a stay-at-home housewife.

A strange choice for a modern young woman. Rather old-fashioned, in Jake's opinion. Made her sound a little odd. He didn't fancy employing odd.

But he would give her a chance. Everyone deserved a chance.

He heard a car pull up outside. A glance at his watch showed it was right on two. She was punctual at least.

Jake stood up and made his way from the study to the front door, arriving in time to unlock the deadbolt just as the doorbell rang. He took a deep breath and opened the door, not sure what to expect.

His breath caught at the sight of a very pretty blonde whose lovely green eyes were looking up at him with a decidedly worried expression. No, not worried. Nervous. The girl was terribly nervous, chewing at her bottom lip and clutching the strap of her black shoulder bag as if it were a lifeline.

He supposed it was only natural that she'd be nervous. Barbara had mentioned that this was the girl's first job interview for her agency. Possibly it was her first job interview ever.

Jake's eyes flicked over the rest of her appearance.

She was wearing dark blue jeans and a cream crocheted top, their snug fit showing a very good figure. Her honey-blonde hair was long and straight, pulled back into a low ponytail. She wasn't wearing make-up, not even lipstick. It pleased Jake that she hadn't dolled herself up like some of the other women he'd interviewed.

'Mr Sanderson?' she asked hesitantly.

Jake's eyebrows rose at the realisation that she didn't recognise him. Which meant she hadn't ever watched his show, or any of the documentaries he'd made over the years.

He didn't know whether to be happy or hurt, which was ironic.

Either way, it was still a positive factor. He definitely didn't want a housekeeper who was a fan.

'Yes, that's me,' he replied, willing now to overlook the fact that she was not only way too young but way too pretty. Jake reasoned that if he hired her, he wouldn't be around her on a daily basis so he wouldn't be in danger of being tempted by her very attractive package. Because, to be honest, it would be seriously hard to ignore those eyes. And that mouth.

Jake dragged his gaze away from it before his mind wandered into R-rated territory.

'And you must be Abby,' he said, smiling a little stiffly.

She smiled back. Not a big smile. A small one. But it showed lovely white teeth behind those luscious lips.

'Yes,' she said simply, then added in a rush, 'it's very good of you to give me an interview.'

'Barbara recommended you highly,' he said.

She seemed startled. 'She did?'

'Indeed, she did. Said she'd dropped in unexpectedly at your home before she signed you up and it was immaculate.'

A soft blush pinked her cheeks. Lord, but she was sweet as well as pretty. Jake liked pretty women, but he wasn't usually attracted to sweet.

Till now...

'I like to keep things nice and neat,' she said.

'Same here,' he said rather brusquely. 'Come in and we'll talk some more.'

'Oh. Right. Yes.' But she didn't move, her lovely eyes wide and unblinking.

Maybe he'd frightened her with his brusqueness. Jake could be very charming, when he chose to be. But he could also be intimidating.

Very charming was definitely not on. But intimidating was not nice either. Best stick to businesslike.

'Perhaps I should give you a tour of the house first,' Jake suggested matter-of-factly, stepping back and waving her inside. 'Show you what you'll be letting yourself in for. You might not want the job, even if I offer it to you.'

'I'm sure I will, Mr Sanderson,' she said and made her way past him into the hallway, where she stopped and stared down. 'Oh, what a lovely floor. I love polished wooden floors.'

'They're hard work to keep clean,' came Jake's blunt comment as he shut the front door behind her.

'I'm not afraid of hard work,' she said, turning to look up at him.

Jake admired the flash of feistiness in her eyes.

It came to him then that he liked this girl. Really *liked* her.

'Excellent,' he said, knowing that he had found his housekeeper at last.

And if it bothered Jake that he also found Abby very desirable, then he determined to ignore it. But he also determined to put things in place so that he would hardly ever see her.

Out of sight was out of mind, after all!

CHAPTER ONE

Twelve months later...

ABBY WAS HUMMING happily as she locked up her neat little weatherboard cottage and headed off to work. She never suffered from Monday-itis. She liked her job. Liked looking after Jake Sanderson's very beautiful house. And looking after Jake Sanderson himself, despite not liking *him* all that much.

Still, Abby would always be grateful to the man for hiring her when she had no current work experience or references.

Frankly, she still could not believe her luck at getting such a cushy position. Aside from the convenience of getting to work—East Balmain wasn't too long a drive from Seven Hills—she was her own boss since Jake was never there when she was. She could do as she pleased; have breaks whenever she wanted; work at her own pace.

Not that she was a slacker. Abby was somewhat of a perfectionist when it came to keeping house. You could eat food off the floors in her own home. And off Jake's by the time she left each day.

Admittedly, when she first arrived on Monday mornings, things could be on the extra messy side. Abby always knew when Jake had had company over the weekend, the kind who stayed the night and didn't bother to lift a finger to pick up dirty wine glasses or load the dishwasher or do anything other than whatever it was his playmates did. The man who'd been voted most popular television personality earlier this year was reputed never to be short of female company.

Abby's sister, Megan, who was addicted to Twitter and gossip magazines, kept Abby well informed about who her boss was currently dating. His latest squeeze was a newsreader from the same television channel that Jake's show aired on. Her name was Olivia, a stunning brunette with big brown eyes and a figure to die for. A smile to die for as well.

There had been a time when Abby would have felt jealous of that smile.

But not any more.

Abby stopped humming abruptly as her tongue

ran over her top teeth, still amazed at how fantastic they felt. Her bottom teeth too.

Of course, porcelain veneers came at a huge cost. Abby still hadn't finished paying off the personal loan she'd taken out to have them done. But really, it had been a case of necessity rather than vanity.

'You need confidence to go back into the workforce after all this time, hon,' her sister had advised. 'Which means you need to do something about your teeth!'

And Megan had been so right. Imagine showing up for an interview with Jake Sanderson the way she'd been. She suffered from fluorosis, a condition which involved an excess of fluoride, caused perhaps by eating fluoride laced toothpaste as a child. She'd loved the taste. Her fluorosis had worsened over the years, the brown stains darkening, pitting her teeth, especially the top ones. Wayne had said she was beautiful the way she was. But Abby had never believed him. So finally, when there'd been no Wayne to object, she'd taken Megan's advice and gone to the dentist.

It had been the best thing she'd ever done, despite putting her into debt.

Not for much longer, though. Each week she

saved every penny she could from her wages, not spending a cent on female fripperies like having her hair and nails done, or even clothes. She just made do with what she had. She also rarely ate out, or went out. If there were no further unexpected expenses—like having to pay for Timmy to have his tonsils out—she would be debt free by Christmas and able to finally start up her travel fund.

Abby had always wanted to see the world, dreams of one day travelling overseas sustaining her when she'd been an unhappy teenager. Okay, so those dreams had been replaced by other dreams when she'd married Wayne, her focus changing to creating a happy family life, the sort of family life that neither she nor Wayne had ever had.

But those dreams had failed to eventuate…

Abby swallowed hard for a few moments, pushing the awful memories aside and forcing herself to focus on dreams which were achievable. And which might make her forget. They did say time healed all wounds. Time, and hopefully travel.

Her dream holiday would encompass at least six months, seeing Europe, Asia and the Americas. There were so many places on her USA bucket list. Niagara Falls. The Grand Canyon. New York.

Which meant of course that one day she'd have to quit her job as Jake's housekeeper.

Megan thought she was crazy to contemplate giving up her cushy job to go tripping around the world.

But Abby didn't agree. She needed to have a dream which looked forward and not back. If she wanted to travel, then she would travel. And to hell with her job as Jake Sanderson's housekeeper. He'd survive without her, and she'd certainly survive without him.

Shortly before nine-thirty, Abby turned into the street which led to Jake's house. The road sloped gently down to the water, and the ferry terminal, most of the houses two-storey terraces which dated back to the early twentieth century. All of them had been renovated at some stage, Balmain being a very desirable address these days, a far cry from its working-class roots.

Jake's house had once been a large corner shop which someone had bought and turned into a house, extending it up and out. Jake had bought it a few years ago. It had come fully furnished in the Balinese style and with everything else he wanted, including a no-lawn backyard, a lap pool with a relaxing water feature and an en suite guest bedroom downstairs.

Apparently, at the time of his purchase, he'd been suffering from some leg injury incurred whilst working overseas and hadn't been capable of climbing stairs for a while. He'd told her all this on the day he'd given her the job, when he'd shown her through the place and explained what he expected her to do. Frankly, he'd spoken to her more that day than in the subsequent twelve months.

Megan was always asking Abby questions about her *oh, so famous and handsome* bachelor boss, not quite believing her sister when Abby said she still knew next to nothing about him other than the basics, which was that he'd once been a famous documentary maker and was now an equally famous television show host. She had recently learnt that he had a favourite uncle named Craig who was a fairly famous foreign correspondent. Abby only knew this because the man himself had recently come to stay for a while after he'd suffered a skiing mishap.

Megan probably knew a lot more about Abby's boss since she avidly watched his programme every day. It was called *Australia at Noon*, a live one-and-a-half-hour programme which focused on celebrity interviews and current affairs, with a bit of variety thrown in—a tried and true formula whose success depended on the popularity of its host. Which Jake Sanderson was. *Very*.

Abby did turn his show on occasionally during her lunch break but found she wasn't as entranced by it—or by its handsome host—as her sister. She found it hard to match his charming television persona with the rather abrupt man who rarely said more than two words to her on the rare occasions their paths crossed.

Not that she cared, as long as he kept on employing her and paying her till her travel fund was full.

This last thought popped into Abby's mind shortly after she let herself into the house and saw what was written in capital letters on the whiteboard in the utility room, where her boss wrote down things he wanted her to do, or buy. He never texted her, seeming to prefer this rather impersonal method of communication.

Will be home around three.
Need to talk to you about something.
Jake

Abby's stomach flipped over, her immediate thought being that she'd done something wrong and he was going to fire her. But then common sense kicked in, Abby reasoning it might be nothing more important than his wanting to show her something which needed doing.

Yes, that was probably it. No need to panic.

But a sense of panic still hovered as time ticked slowly away that day. Meanwhile, Abby worked like a demon so that by the time three o'clock came around every room and surface in Jake's house was clean and shining. All the pictures and side tables had been dusted. The washing had been done and dried, the master bed remade with clean sheets and fresh towels hung in the main bathroom. Even the courtyard had been swept, and a few of the pavers scrubbed where some red wine had been spilled. She hadn't had a break, eating her lunch on the go.

At ten to three Abby removed her cleaning gloves and tidied her hair, brushing it before putting it back up into her usual ponytail. She always wore jeans and trainers to work, with a T-shirt in the warm weather and a sweater in the cold. Today's jeans were old and faded and a bit loose. Her black T-shirt was slightly too big for her as well. She'd lost weight lately, courtesy of her banning chocolate and ice cream from her diet.

Abby sighed at her reflection in the laundry mirror. She wished she looked better. She would have taken more trouble with her appearance this morning if she'd known she was going to have a meeting with her boss. But how could she have known? She hadn't seen him for weeks. Still, she really should go out and buy herself a few new things. Jeans and T-shirts didn't cost much at Kmart.

Three o'clock came and went without any sign of Jake. After ten minutes she wondered if she should text him. She did have his phone number but he'd made it clear from the start that she wasn't to bother him that way, except in an emergency.

Him being late was hardly an emergency. Still, if he hadn't arrived by three-thirty she would text him. Meanwhile, she hurried to the kitchen and put on the kettle.

CHAPTER TWO

JAKE STEPPED OUT onto the deck of the ferry and scooped in several deep breaths. His stomach was still tied up in knots. He'd done his best with his show today, but his mind hadn't been on the job. Not that he cared. Frankly, he wouldn't care if he never did another show. Andrew had stood in for him as host last Friday and the ratings were just fine. No one was indispensable in the entertainment game.

Jake contemplated letting Andrew take over for a week or two whilst he took a well-needed break. He'd jump at the chance, ambitious young buck that he was. Alternately, he might sell the show lock, stock and barrel and do something else with his life. Harvest Productions had been sniffing around for ages. If he could talk Sebastian into making him a half decent offer, he just might take him up on it.

Though maybe not…

Jake ran his fingers through his hair in total

frustration. Damn it. He hadn't felt this indecisive in years. Of course he knew the reason. He just didn't like facing it. Sighing, he made his way over to the railing and stood there, staring out at the water.

Sydney Harbour on a clear calm day in spring was a sight to behold. But Jake wasn't in the mood for admiring his surroundings. Or even noticing them.

Closing his eyes, he surrendered to the grief which he'd had to put on hold today whilst he did the show, and which he'd been struggling to contain for several days.

Jake still could not believe that his uncle was actually dead. Not even the funeral last Friday had made it real. He could not picture Craig in that coffin. Could not conceive of the fact that he would never see the man again. Would not talk to him again. Or drink with him. Or anything at all with him.

Craig had been much more than an uncle to Jake. He'd been his mentor and his friend. His idol, too. Even as a boy, Jake had admired the way his uncle lived his life.

Craig hadn't gone down the traditional route, getting a nine-to-five job then marrying and having children. He'd become a foreign correspondent, travelling the world to all the wildly exotic and sometimes dangerous places which fired Jake's imagination. He'd also stayed single, explaining once to a teenage Jake that for him to marry would be cruel to the woman, and to any children they had because he would neglect them shamelessly.

There'd been women, of course. Lots of women. Beautiful, exciting women who'd graced the dashingly handsome Craig Sanderson's bed but who knew never to expect any more than his highly stimulating company.

Jake had decided long before he left university with his communications degree that that was the life for him. No way was he going to follow in his father's footsteps. Craig's only brother had married before he was twenty, when his even younger girlfriend fell pregnant, then worked himself to death—literally—to support his ever-increasing brood.

Jake couldn't think of anything worse. He could not recall his father—when he was alive—having any time to himself. Everything he'd done had been for his family.

When his dad died of a coronary at the age of forty-seven, Jake had been heartbroken but more determined than ever to embrace bachelorhood as well as a job which he loved and not one he was compelled to do just to pay the bills and put food on the table.

Jake had been true to his resolve. He'd spent his twenties making documentaries in far-flung corners of the world, earning a small fortune at the same time. He'd still be overseas, living that life, if a run-in with a group of rebels in war-torn Africa hadn't forced his life into a different direction.

Working in television was tame by comparison, but it had its moments. Jake couldn't really complain.

Admittedly, since he'd stopped flitting from country to country and city to city, Jake had given up one-night stands and fleeting flings in favour of longer relationships. If you could call a few months long, that was. His current girlfriend was a career-orientated and highly independent woman who was great company, great in bed and knew better than to pressure him for marriage or, God forbid, a baby. Olivia had assured him on their first date that she wouldn't get bitten by the biological clock bug like his last girlfriend. The only responsibility Jake wanted in life was paying his own personal bills.

Which was exactly the way things had been...

till the solicitor for Craig's estate had dropped his bombshell at the wake.

Jake already knew he'd been left the bulk of his uncle's estate, Craig having given him a copy of his will for safekeeping. What he hadn't known was that Craig had summoned his solicitor to his bedside a few days before his death and given him a letter for Jake, to be delivered after his funeral.

Jake pulled the letter out of his pocket, unfolded it and read it for the umpteenth time.

Dear Jake

Hope you aren't angry with me for not telling you about my illness, but there was nothing anyone could do and I do so hate pity. I had a good life, my only regret being that I didn't go out with more style. A bullet or a bomb would have been much more me.

But on to the reason for this letter. Jake, there's something I want you to do for me. Last July, when I stayed at your place after I bunged up my knee, I got to know your very nice housekeeper quite well. Abby was extra kind to me and went over and above the call of duty to make my stay both comfortable and enjoyable. And, no, nothing un-

*toward happened between us. She's not that
sort of girl.*

*Anyway, on to my request. I didn't want to
add a codicil to my will. Too much trouble
at this stage. Still, what I would like, Jake,
is for you to buy Abby a new car to replace
that appalling bomb she drives. Something
small and stylish but with a long warranty.*

*I also want you to give her twenty-five
thousand dollars out of your considerable
inheritance to go towards her travel fund.
Please insist that she not use it for any other
purpose. Don't let her give it away to any of
those free-loading relatives of hers.*

*I have every confidence that you will do
this for me. You're a good man. And not a
greedy one. Give Abby my love and tell her
not to wait too long to see the world. Life is
meant to be lived.*

*The same goes for you, my boy. I'll be
watching over you from above.*
Your Uncle Craig

Jake closed his eyes as he folded the letter, a
huge lump having formed in his throat.

'Damn it, Craig,' he ground out, his heart
squeezing tight with grief. 'You should have told

me you were ill. I could have been there for you the way you always were for me. You shouldn't have had to die alone.'

And you should have just put a damned codicil in your will, came the added thought, grief finally giving way to exasperation.

It was impossible not to do what Craig asked, Jake accepted as he shoved the letter back in his pocket. But it annoyed him all the same.

It wasn't a question of money. He had plenty of money. It was the fact that fulfilling his uncle's deathbed wishes would force him into Abby's personal space—and company—something he'd been careful to avoid ever since he'd hired her.

Because let's face it, Jake, you fancy her even more now than ever.

But he could see no way out. He would just have to gird his loins and endure!

CHAPTER THREE

AT TWENTY PAST THREE Abby's boss finally showed up, looking slightly harassed but still very handsome in a smart grey suit and a crisp white shirt which highlighted his dark hair, olive complexion and deep blue eyes.

Even Abby had to admit that in the flesh her boss was a hunk. But she'd never been blindly attracted to a man on looks alone. Handsome is as handsome does, in her opinion. What attracted her most in the opposite sex was kindness and gentleness, qualities which Wayne had had in spades.

'Sorry I'm late,' Jake said as he strode into the kitchen, where Abby was making herself coffee. 'Damned ferry was running late. Could I trouble you for some coffee? Black, with no sugar,' he ordered as he slid on to one of the kitchen stools, reefing off his tie at the same time.

Abby wanted to scream at him. Didn't he

know how stressed out she was? But she held her tongue and made him the darned coffee.

'So what did you want to talk to me about?' she asked as soon as she'd placed his mug in front of him. She stayed standing on the other side of the breakfast bar, not daring to pick up her own coffee yet for fear of spilling it.

His forehead bunched in a frown, which only added to her discomfort.

'You're going to fire me, aren't you?' she blurted out.

His head shot up, his dark brows arching. 'What? No. No, of course not! Good God, is that what you thought this was about?'

She just shook her head at him. 'I didn't know what to think.'

'Why on earth would I want to fire you? You are the best housekeeper a man could have. I'm sorry if you thought that.'

Abby found herself flushing at his compliment. And his apology. Relief swamped her as well. She didn't want to lose this job. Not for a good while yet.

'It's to do with Craig's will,' Jake said abruptly.

'Craig's *will*?' she repeated, feeling somewhat confused. 'Are you talking about your uncle

Craig, the man who stayed here for a while during the winter?'

It had been back in July, she recalled, about four months ago.

'Yes. The thing is, Abby, he's left you something in his will.'

Abby just stared at Jake, shock joining her confusion. 'Are you saying that he's *dead*?'

'What? Oh. Yes. Yes, he died last week. Incurable cancer,' he finished up with a heavy sigh.

'But…but that's impossible! I mean, he was so *alive* not that long ago.'

'Tell me about it,' Jake said as he swept an agitated hand through his hair. 'It came as a shock to me as well. I gather he found out during an MRI for his busted knee about the cancer. But he never told anyone, not even me. And we were very close. I knew nothing about his illness till his solicitor rang and told me he'd passed away.'

Abby found it hard to understand what he was saying. 'You mean you weren't with him when he died?'

'No. No one was, other than the palliative care nurse. He'd booked himself into a hospice without telling anyone.'

'But that's terrible!' Abby declared heatedly, upset that anyone would choose to die like that.

Jake's shrug carried a weary resignation. 'It was what he wanted. I'm surprised you didn't hear about his death. It was all over the news at the weekend. He was quite famous.'

'I… I don't often watch the news.'

'I see.'

She wanted to ask him why he hadn't told her himself, but of course why would he? She wasn't a relative, or a friend. He wouldn't have known how much she'd enjoyed the time she'd spent with his uncle whilst he'd stayed here.

Craig had been a fascinating individual, highly intelligent, widely travelled and very well read. He'd been incredibly nice to her, showing an interest in her as a person and not just some kind of maid. The day before he'd left, he'd given her a list of ten books which he said everybody— especially young women—should read. She was still slowly working her way through them. They were the reason she didn't watch the news much any more, and why she hadn't seen the report of his death.

Tears flooded her eyes at the realisation that this very nice man was actually dead.

'He…he said he was going away to have a holiday.' Abby's voice caught at the memory.

'He told me the same thing,' Jake said.

'Instead he went away to die,' she choked out. 'Alone...'

Abby couldn't think of anything sadder than dying alone. It was the main thing which haunted her about Wayne's death. That he'd been all alone, out there in the ocean, with the storm raging around him and little chance of being rescued. Had he lost all hope in the end? Had despair engulfed him in the moments before he drowned?

Suddenly, a huge wave of grief overwhelmed her, emotional distress welling up in Abby till it could not be contained. Tears filled her eyes so quickly they spilled over and ran down her cheeks.

When a sob escaped her throat, Jake stared at her with a look of horror.

Embarrassment flooded in but there was no stopping her now. When more sobs racked her body, all Abby could do was bury her face in her hands. She simply couldn't bear to witness her boss watching her whilst she wept her heart out. No doubt she was making a fool of herself. No doubt he thought she was a typically sentimental female to cry over a man she hardly knew.

The feel of strong male arms suddenly pulling

her into a comforting embrace shocked Abby rigid. She certainly hadn't expected a hug. Not from her very aloof boss. Unfortunately, his uncharacteristic kindness only made her weep all the more.

'There, there,' he said, patting her back as she clasped the lapels of his suit jacket and sobbed into his shirt. 'No need to cry. Craig had a good life, with no regrets. He wouldn't want you crying over him. Craig wasn't one for tears.'

Abby could hardly explain that it wasn't just Craig's death which had set her off, but the *way* he'd died. All alone.

Oh, God...

Abby was gritting her teeth and doing her best to pull herself together when Jake stopped patting her back and slid his arms right around her, holding her quite close. No doubt he was still just trying to comfort her but for some reason Abby no longer felt comforted. She felt very *dis*comforted. Because she *liked* him hugging her like that. She liked it a lot. The urge to slide her own arms around his back was acute. She wanted to hug him back, wanted to bury herself in the solid warmth of his very male body and...and...

And what, Abby? Make an even bigger fool of yourself? For pity's sake, get a grip, girl.

Taking a deep gathering breath, Abby lurched backwards, releasing the lapels of Jake's jacket as she gulped down a sob of shame.

'I'm so sorry,' she choked out, her face flushing as she spun away from him and grabbed a handful of tissues from the box on the kitchen counter, not saying another word till she'd blown her nose and composed herself. She did note rather ruefully, however, that Jake didn't wait long to hurry back to the other side of the breakfast bar.

Her groan carried more shame. 'I've embarrassed you, I can see. It's just that… Oh, never mind.' Her fisted right hand came up to rub agitatedly at her mouth. For a moment she was tempted to confide in Jake about Wayne's tragic death. But only for a moment. Maybe, if he'd been any other kind of man she might have explained why she'd been so upset at the news of his uncle dying alone like that. But Jake didn't invite confidences. Why, he'd never even asked her how her husband had died!

Despite his hug just now, Jake didn't really care about her. She was just his employee, hired to look after his house. His housekeeper. A glorified cleaner, if truth be told.

Craig hadn't treated her like that. He'd been genuinely interested in her life. Not that she'd told Jake's uncle the total truth. Abby had become masterful at blotting out the really painful parts in her past. Talking about them wouldn't have achieved anything, anyway.

'The thing is,' she went on, compelled to make some excuse for her emotional display, 'I really liked your uncle a lot.'

'He must have liked you a lot too,' Jake replied.

'Well, yes,' she said slowly. 'He seemed to.'

'You haven't asked me what he left you,' Jake went on, his eyes on her.

'What? Oh... Some books, I suppose.'

Jake frowned at her. 'No, no books,' he said. 'Nothing as mundane as that.'

'Then what?' she asked, perplexed.

'To be honest, he didn't leave you anything directly. He left a letter for me with instructions of what he wants you to have.'

She blinked, then frowned. 'That sounds... weird.'

'Yes, I thought so too,' he agreed drily. 'But Craig was never a conventional man. Look, why don't we both drink our coffee before it gets cold? Then, afterwards, I'll fill you in on everything.'

When Jake picked up his coffee mug, Abby did likewise, sipping slowly and thoughtfully. A hot drink always calmed her. And brother, she needed calming after that crazy moment when she'd almost hugged her boss back.

'I would have liked to go to his funeral,' she said after a suitably calming minute or two. 'Was he buried or cremated?'

'Buried,' he said.

'Where?' she asked.

Jake's face looked grim as he put down his coffee. 'Rookwood Cemetery.'

She wasn't sure where that was. She didn't have a GPS in the ute and often got lost. 'I'd like to go and visit his grave some time. Pay my respects. Say a prayer or two. Would you take me?' she asked him before she could think better of it.

Jake's sigh suggested that was the last thing he wanted to do.

'Okay,' he said with a resigned shrug. 'But I can't go till next Saturday. In the meantime, wouldn't you like to hear about what Craig wanted me to give you?'

'Oh, yes. What is it?'

'Well, first of all he wants me to buy you a new car. Something small and stylish, with a decent warranty.'

Shock at this news was swiftly followed by confusion.

'But that doesn't seem right,' she said. 'As much as I would love a new car, why should he ask *you* to pay for such a thing?'

'It's basically Craig's money, Abby. He left most of his estate to me. Trust me when I say that my inheritance was considerable. So it's no hardship on me to spend a seriously small portion of it on you.'

'But why didn't he just leave some money to me in his will to buy my own car?'

'I have no idea. It might have been simpler all round if he'd done that. Apparently, he was worried that you might not spend it on yourself—that you might give it away to relatives.'

'Oh, dear,' she said, embarrassed. 'I suppose it's because I told him about paying for Timmy's operation.'

'No. He didn't mention anything specific. Who's Timmy?'

'My sister's little boy. She's a single mum and doesn't have any private health insurance. Timmy needed his tonsils out but would have had to wait eighteen months to have it done. She couldn't afford the operation so I paid for it to be done privately.'

'I see,' he said, his tone sceptical.

A degree of anger pushed aside Abby's embarrassment. 'Please don't think my sister's a user because she's not. She's doing the best she can under the circumstances. Megan didn't ask me to pay for Timmy's operation. That was *my* idea. She won't come and live with me, even though I said she wouldn't have to pay any rent. Your uncle got the wrong idea.'

'Possibly, but that's irrelevant now. I have no alternative but to follow through with Craig's dying wishes. He was most specific in his letter about what he wanted me to buy for you. A new car is the first cab off the rank. Then he wants me to give you twenty-five thousand dollars. For your travel fund, he said.'

Abby's mouth dropped open. 'Twenty-five thousand! But…but that's way too much. What will people think?'

'Who cares what they think?' came his arrogantly dismissive comment. 'And who are *they*?'

'My sister for starters. She'll think I've done something I shouldn't have with your uncle to get him to leave me all that money.'

'Really. Such as what?'

'You know what,' Abby shot back.

'True,' he said drily. 'In that case I suggest you don't tell her about your unexpected windfall.'

Abby gave a snorting laugh. 'Hard to hide a brand-new car.'

'True again. So what do you want me to do, Abby? Go against my uncle's wishes? Forget everything?'

She looked at him with pained eyes. 'I couldn't do that. I don't care so much about the new car, but I couldn't turn down the travel fund money. It's my dearest wish to go overseas and see the world. And I'd like to go before I get too old.'

Jake laughed. 'You're hardly ancient, Abby.'

'I might be by the time I save up twenty-five thousand dollars.'

He seemed startled by this statement. 'Do I pay you that poorly?'

'No. But I have a house and a lot of bills.' And the remainder of a debt for porcelain veneers.

Jake frowned. 'You have a mortgage?'

'No. My husband's life insurance paid that off. But I still have a lot of bills. Maintaining a house is expensive.'

'Tell me about it,' he said with the first hint of a smile that day. He really wasn't much of a smiler. Not with her, anyway. He smiled on television a lot though. Abby wished he would smile more. It really transformed his face from cardboard handsome into a likeable human being.

Unfortunately, his smile also did things to Abby which she was finding hard to process. Her stomach curled over and she found herself staring at his mouth and thinking totally unacceptable things. Like what would it be like to be kissed by him? And not just on her mouth.

Lord, but this wasn't like her. She didn't even enjoy sex that much, unlike her sister, who couldn't live without it. Sex with Wayne had been okay, but nothing to write home about. She'd done it whenever he wanted, more for him than herself, because she'd loved him so much. In her mind, making love was a natural part of loving. Of marriage. She'd never been into sex for sex's sake.

Why then was she looking at her boss and thinking that here was a man who just might change her mind on that subject?

Not that she'd ever have the chance to find out. Not only did he have a gorgeous girlfriend but he was totally off-limits. He was her boss, for heaven's sake! On top of that, he clearly didn't fancy her. A girl knew when a man fancied her and Jake definitely didn't.

Her eyes dropped from his to her near empty coffee cup.

'I'm still finding it hard to believe all this,' she

said, glancing up again once she had her way-ward thoughts under control. 'In one way it's like a dream come true. But I still can't get over your uncle dying like that. And all alone.'

'Indeed,' Jake said, that hint of a smile dis-appearing as quickly as it had come. 'I've been thinking,' he went on, his face very businesslike again. 'I'll put next Saturday aside so that I can take you to visit Craig's grave in the morning, then we'll go on and buy you a car afterwards. It's not far from Rookwood Cemetery out to the major dealerships at Parramatta. Do you trust me to pick out a car for you, or do you want to choose one yourself?'

'Well, I… I don't know,' she stammered, star-tled by how quickly he wanted to organise ev-erything. 'I'm not much of a car buff. But if it's going to be mine I think I would like to look up a few possibilities on the internet.'

'It's a good idea to buy something that is cheap to repair,' he advised firmly. 'I would suggest you look at the Japanese cars. Or the Korean ones.'

'All right,' she agreed. He seemed to know what he was talking about, whereas she was pretty ignorant when it came to cars.

'And what bank account would you like the

twenty-five thousand put into? The same one your salary goes into, or do you want to start up a special travel fund account?'

Abby was taken by surprise when her chin began to quiver. But really today had all been a bit much.

'Don't you dare start crying again,' he commanded.

Abby bit her bottom lip and blinked madly.

'Sorry,' she muttered through gritted teeth. 'I'm not usually a cry baby.' Which was true. Nowadays, Abby kept her emotions under tight control. There had been a time when she'd cried too much. And too often. But no longer.

Lifting her chin, she speared her boss with a dry-eyed and rather rebellious glare.

'Good,' Jake snapped, making Abby want to hit him. How on earth she could have been sexually attracted to this man—even for a moment— was beyond her.

'You should go home,' he went on in that same brusque manner. 'You look tired. Ring me when you've decided on the brand of car and we'll make arrangements for Saturday. You can tell me then what account you want the money put into.'

'All right. Bye then,' Abby went on rather sharply, gathering up her things and taking off before she could say or do something which might jeopardise her job. Or Craig's remarkable legacies.

She almost slammed the front door, just getting control of her temper in time. She did slam the door on the ute and accelerated off faster than her usual sedate speed. But she soon slowed down, telling herself not to be so silly. No point risking her life because her boss was a pain in the butt.

Think about your new car, she told herself. *And all that lovely money.*

Abby sighed. Yes, it was sad that Craig was dead, but life went on, as she very well knew. You had to search for the positives in life or you would go mad.

Another thought suddenly came to Abby which made her wince. How much of this was she going to tell Megan? As she'd said to Jake, you couldn't hide a new car. But perhaps it would be best if she didn't tell her sister about the money. It might make her jealous and, yes, suspicious.

Abby pulled a face at herself in the rear-view mirror. She hated lying to Megan but she just might have to. Oh, dear. Even when things took a turn for the better, life wasn't easy.

CHAPTER FOUR

'YOU HANDLED THAT WELL,' Jake growled as he pulled a bottle of red at random out of his wine rack. 'I love the way you kept her at a distance.'

Still, what could he do when she started crying like that? Common sense demanded he do nothing. But common decency insisted that he comfort her.

Big mistake.

The moment he'd taken her in his arms, all those good intentions of his dissolved in the face of a desire so strong it took every ounce of will-power not to pull her even closer than he had. He didn't want to pat her damned back. Or utter soothing words. He wanted to tip up her chin and kiss the tears from her lovely face.

Thank God he hadn't given in to that desire. Because she would not have surrendered to him as she did in his darkest dreams. She would have slapped him, then resigned as his housekeeper.

Abby didn't particularly like him. That, he knew.

Which should have been a relief, given his resolve never to act on his secret desire for her. Instead he felt peeved by her indifference. And jealous of her obvious affection for Craig. Which was all perverse, given his own decision not to have anything to do with her on a personal level, a decision which fate—courtesy of his uncle—had now blown out of the water. Next Saturday morning he would be *personally* escorting Abby to Craig's graveside, then afterwards he would be *personally* buying her a car.

That was all pretty personal, in his opinion.

But there was no way out, Jake accepted bleakly as he gazed down at the label of the bottle he'd pulled out and saw it was one of his favourites. A Shiraz from the Clare Valley. Good. Because he needed to get drunk. And he might as well do so on a favourite tipple rather than rubbish.

Not that he ever bought rubbish, he admitted as he poured himself his first glass. Long gone were the days when he drank rough red from casks. Hell, he hadn't done that since his university days. And yet they had been good days. Happy days. Carefree days.

Nothing like today, Jake thought ruefully as he lifted the glass to his lips for a deep swallow.

Today would not go down as good. Or happy. Or carefree. Today was…what?

He wasn't sure how to describe it.

Dangerous came to mind. And not in a good way. Jake had enjoyed danger in his life at times. But this was a different kind of danger. This wasn't physical danger. This involved his emotions. Intense, uncontrollable emotions.

Jake didn't like intense, uncontrollable emotions. They made you do things which never ended well.

Jake carried the glass and the bottle out to his courtyard, where he placed the bottle on the small circular glass table he liked best then sat down in the chair next to it.

When his phone rang, he saw that it was Olivia.

He didn't want to talk to Olivia just now. He didn't want to talk to anyone. So he just turned off the phone and went back to drinking his wine.

CHAPTER FIVE

WITHIN SECONDS OF arriving home Abby rang Megan, not wanting to procrastinate over the call. Megan would only be even more suspicious if she waited too long to give her the good news.

'Hi there, kiddo,' Megan answered, a term of endearment which often led people to think Megan was the older sister. And whilst there wasn't much between them, Abby was actually older by fifteen months.

Abby had already decided that the best way to play this was to sound very happy about it. And she *was* happy. Just a bit wary about her sister's reaction.

'You'll never guess what's happened,' Abby said brightly as she dumped her bag on the floor and plonked herself into a nearby armchair.

'Something good by the sound of things.'

'Unbelievably good!' And she launched into an explanation of the day's events. As planned, she left out the part about the travel fund money and only mentioned the new car. Naturally, she didn't include the bit about her bursting into tears and Jake hugging her.

Megan exclaimed a shocked, 'No!' at the news about the new car, but thankfully didn't make any sarcastic crack about what Abby might have done with Jake's uncle to deserve such an incredibly generous gift. Things might have been different, however, if she'd mentioned the twenty-five thousand dollars as well. Though possibly not. Maybe Megan instinctively knew that Abby would never do anything sexual with a man she didn't love. Wayne had been her first and only lover because he was the first and only man she'd ever loved.

'Aren't you a lucky duck?' Megan said without a trace of jealousy in her voice. 'A brand-new car! And you don't even have to wait for probate to come through, since your hunky boss is buying you the car himself. This Saturday, you said?'

'Yes. This Saturday.'

'It's a wonderful gift. Especially when you hardly knew his uncle. But perhaps not so much if he was filthy rich. Was he filthy rich?'

'He must have been. Jake said he'd inherited

heaps. That's why he doesn't mind forking out the money for me for a car.'

'Oh, right. Still, it's nice of him to do that. He's not legally obliged to, I would imagine.'

'Probably not, but he said he would never go against his uncle's deathbed wishes.'

'Did you see this letter his uncle left him?'

'Well, no, but why would he lie about something like that?'

'Maybe he fancies you.'

'Oh, don't be ridiculous! Why would he fancy someone like me when he has that gorgeous girl-friend? I've been thinking, Megan, since I'm getting a new car, would you like the ute? I know it's done a good few miles but it goes really well. Wayne put a new engine in it not long before he died.'

'Oh, I'd *love* it. Thanks, Abby.'

'Jake is going to take me to see his uncle's grave as well,' she blurted out before she could think better of it.

The silence at the other end of the line was telling.

'Oh, is he?' Megan said at long last in one of her knowing voices. 'And why is he doing that?'

'Because I asked him to,' Abby said, angry with herself. 'And, before you jump to conclusions, we're just dropping in at the cemetery on the way to the car yards at Parramatta. It's hardly out of his way. And you are so wrong about his fancying me.'

Megan laughed. 'We'll see, hon. We'll see.'

'Oh, for pity's sake.'

'You've always underestimated your looks, Abby. Even when your teeth were not great, you were gorgeous. Now that you've had them fixed, you're a knockout. And your figure is to die for.'

'Oh, go on with you!'

'No, I mean it. Your fantastic figure was one of the reasons Wayne was so possessive of you. And why he didn't want you to work after you were married. Because he didn't want other men lusting after you.'

Abby's first reaction was to hotly deny what Megan said. But in her heart of hearts she knew it was true. Wayne had been very possessive of her. Right from the start, he'd wanted her all to himself. Which had suited Abby fine. All she'd wanted back then was to be Wayne's wife, plus the mother of his children. She'd been only too happy to stop work and not have to face the world every day with her horrible teeth. Not so happy, however, as the years had passed and the nursery remained empty.

'That's probably the reason he wouldn't pay for you to get your teeth fixed,' Megan continued. 'Because he was afraid you'd be too beautiful and he'd lose you to another man.'

'That's ridiculous!' Abby protested. 'The reason I didn't get my teeth fixed back then was because it's very expensive and we had a huge mortgage. Besides, Wayne already loved me, even with my horrid teeth. As for being too beautiful, please don't make me laugh. Even if by some miracle I'd become the most beautiful woman in the world, I would never have left Wayne, no matter what. I loved him.'

'Did you, Abby? Or did you just love that he loved you with the kind of crazy obsession which can be oh, so flattering?'

'I did so love Wayne,' she insisted. 'Very much. We would have been happy together if we'd had children.'

Megan sighed. 'If you say so, Abby.'

'I do say so. Now, I do not wish to discuss Wayne any more, thank you. I didn't realise how much you disliked him.'

'I didn't dislike him. I just didn't think he was good enough for you. You deserved someone better.'

Abby didn't know whether to feel flattered

or frustrated. 'Such as who, Megan? Prince Charming?'

'Yeah, why not? And let me tell you something else, kiddo. If you bought some new clothes and put on some make-up occasionally, you would be so hot that every man you met would be drooling. And that includes your handsome hunk of a boss.'

Abby didn't like to tell Megan that she was being delusional—about Jake at least—so she just laughed.

'Yeah, you can laugh if you like. Just you wait and see. Speaking of your boss, did you happen to watch his show today?'

'Hardly. I was too busy cleaning his house.'

'He interviewed Maddie Hanks. You know, the latest Aussie actress who's made it big in Hollywood?'

'I know who you mean. She was in that biblical epic. Played a slave girl.'

'Yeah, that's the one. Well, she was flirting with Jake big time. And brother, she is stunning. He seemed very taken with her. Couldn't keep his eyes off her cleavage. Though I don't think her boobs are real. Anyway, I wouldn't mind betting they get together in the near future.'

Abby rolled her eyes. Truly, her sister was so

addicted to gossip that she saw scandalous behaviour everywhere. 'Jake already has a gorgeous girlfriend,' she pointed out. 'That newsreader. Remember?'

'Huh! That won't stop him getting into Miss Hanks's pants.'

'He's not like that,' Abby said sharply.

'Oh, really? And how would you know, Miss I-Know-Nothing-Personal-About-My-Hunk-of-a-Boss? Did something else happen today that you didn't tell me about?'

'No,' she denied, blanking the hug out of her mind. 'Look, I'm not overly fond of the man, but he's not some sleazebag.'

'Wow. He's sure got you fooled. All men can be sleazebags if the right temptation comes along.'

Abby just shook her head. 'Truly, Megan, you are such a cynic when it comes to men.'

'I have good reason to be.'

This *was* true. Timmy's father hadn't been the first man in Megan's life to treat her badly. She'd met a few since becoming a single mother who'd wined and dined her till they got what they wanted before dumping her as cruelly as the cowardly creep who'd got her pregnant then disappeared once he discovered fatherhood was too much commitment for him.

'I hope you're going to make yourself present-able when your boss takes you out on Saturday,' Megan said.

'It's not a date, Megan.'

'You still want to look a bit nicer than you do when you clean his house.'

'I will do my best.'

'Good. Gosh, wait till Jan hears all this. She's going to be green with envy.'

Jan was Megan's next-door neighbour, a single mother like Megan. She was one of the reasons Megan wouldn't come to live with Abby, because she didn't want to leave her best friend. Abby wasn't overly keen on Jan, but she'd been a good friend to Megan and had a similar personality. Both were very easy-going but extremely untidy. Abby had been somewhat relieved when Megan knocked back her offer for her and Timmy to come live with her. Their messy lifestyle would have driven her mad within a week.

'Jan's sure to think I did something suspect with Jake's uncle,' Abby said drily.

'Nah. Now if it was *me*.'

Abby smiled. 'Come on, Megan, you're not as bad as you pretend to be.'

'Yeah, I am. Not everyone is as saint-like as you, sweetie. Though, to give you credit, being a goody-two-shoes got you somewhere this time. I dare say you waited on that rich old bastard hand and foot. You probably even baked him those delicious peanut butter cookies of yours.'

Abby fell silent with guilty embarrassment. She *had* made a fuss of Jake's uncle. But, at the time, it had been ages since her nurturing side had had an opportunity to flourish. Looking after Jake's house was a rather impersonal job. It had been so satisfying to bake cookies for a real man and, yes, watch him eat them with relish. She'd enjoyed it all immensely.

'You did, didn't you?' Megan said with laughter in her voice. 'No wonder he thought of you when he was dying. Those cookies of yours are super-yummy. Though way too fattening. I refuse to let you make me any more. Though Timmy wouldn't mind some, when you have your next baking session. I have to go and get the little devil himself now. He's been playing next door. Ring me tomorrow night. Gotta go. Love ya.'

'You too.'

After Abby clicked off her phone she just sat there, thinking about some of the things Megan had said about her marriage to Wayne. It was true that her husband had loved her more than she'd loved him. But she *had* loved him. Okay, not with a grand passion. Her feelings for Wayne had been based more on a deep friendship and eternal gratitude rather than the kind of wild sexual yearnings which some people obviously experienced.

Abby supposed she *had* been flattered by Wayne's fiercely possessive love. And his insatiable desire for her. After her second miscarriage, she'd wanted to take her doctor's advice to go on the Pill and give her body a rest. But no, Wayne had refused to countenance that idea, saying he didn't like to interfere with nature. He'd promised instead to abstain from sex for a while but, of course, that hadn't lasted for long. He'd never been able to control his desire for her and she'd never felt good about refusing him, mostly because she knew how much he seemed to need it.

Abby liked the kissing and cuddling part of lovemaking—she'd loved being wrapped in Wayne's strong arms—but she'd never felt any urgent need for the sex act itself, unlike Megan, who claimed she couldn't live without it. It had never really bothered Abby that she didn't come during lovemaking. It had bothered Wayne, however, so after a while she had just faked it.

She hadn't had to fake falling pregnant, however, and a few months after her second miscarriage she'd been pregnant again. But, once again, she'd miscarried at the three months stage. After that, she'd gone on the Pill without discussing it with Wayne, and she was still taking it long after her husband was gone, mainly because she'd discovered it saved her from premenstrual tension.

It felt good, Abby realised, to finally be in control of her body and, yes, her life. She'd been gutted by Wayne's tragic death, had taken months to get over it. But in the end she'd picked herself up and moved on.

Now, because of Craig's wonderful kindness and generosity, she would be able to move on some more. And Jake would find another housekeeper easily enough.

Thinking of Jake reminded Abby of what Megan had said about him, and about men in general. Abby had to admit that *her* view of the opposite sex was possibly narrower than her sister's. But she wasn't stupid. She was sure she would recognise a sleazebag when she came across one. And Jake Sanderson was no sleazebag.

But that was possibly the only good point of his character. Abby could see that he had a tendency towards arrogance and self-absorption. Neither was he into commitment, hence his never-ending parade of beautiful girlfriends. But that didn't mean he would be a cheater. She couldn't imagine him having sex with some flashy, fly-by-night actress whilst he was dating that truly gorgeous newsreader.

Abby would be utterly disgusted if she ever found out he *had* done something like that. Not that it was any of her business what her boss did in his private and personal life. Still, it bothered her a bit, thinking that he could be, right at this moment, meeting up with Maddie Hanks somewhere in the city then bringing her back to his place for the night.

It occurred to Abby that she would know within a minute of arriving at his house tomorrow morning if he'd had a new woman stay overnight. Abby knew his current girlfriend's smell because she recognised the perfume. It was a heavy musky scent which didn't wear off easily. During the last few weeks Abby had smelled that perfume every couple of days, and almost always on a Monday after the weekend.

But not *this* Monday morning, she suddenly realised. Which led her to wonder if maybe they'd split up. Maybe that was why he'd been giving

Maddie Hanks the eye on his show today. Men like Jake didn't go without sex for long. Because they didn't have to. Women threw themselves at famous men in droves—beautiful, sexy, success-ful women who knew everything there was to know about lovemaking and never had to fake a thing.

A very rude word burst from Abby's lips as she stood up abruptly then marched into her im-maculate little kitchen, where she snapped on the kettle then yanked open the freezer, which was full of frozen meals for one.

Still feeling decidedly disgruntled, she grabbed a chilli con carne and shoved it into the micro-wave to reheat, telling herself all the while that her boss's sex life was definitely none of her business.

'He can sleep with whomever he damned well likes,' she said in a tone quite uncharacteristic of her usual serene self. 'Just so long as he delivers everything he promised me today!'

CHAPTER SIX

JAKE LEFT IT until nine that evening to ring Olivia back, having learnt from experience that it was never wise to ring her before she'd been home for a while after work. After reading the news from six till seven, Olivia usually went for a de-stressing drink down near the quay before catching the Manly ferry home.

Her phone rang several times before she picked up.

'Well, hello, stranger,' she answered waspishly. 'Why didn't you answer when I rang you earlier?'

'I didn't feel like talking,' he said with blunt honesty.

'Are you upset with me for not going to your uncle's funeral?'

'No,' he told her with equal honesty. 'I didn't expect you to cancel your arrangements when they'd been organised weeks before Craig died.'

Olivia and five of her girlfriends had driven

up to a resort in the Blue Mountains on the Friday for a hen party for one of the girls, who was getting married shortly.

'I was home by eight last night,' Olivia pointed out tartly. 'Why didn't you ring? I was waiting for your call. Or your text. Or something.'

Jake was totally taken aback. They didn't have the kind of relationship where they called and texted each other all the time. They were lovers, but not in love.

'You told me you were turning off your phone for the weekend,' he reminded her. 'Nothing stopped you ringing me when you got home last night.'

'I was tired.'

'More likely hungover.'

'Yes,' she admitted grudgingly. 'That, too. But you still could have contacted me this morning.'

'Come now, Olivia. You know I'm busy on weekday mornings, getting ready for my show.'

'Ah, yes. Your show,' she said in a tone which had a decided edge to it. 'I happened to watch your show today...'

'And?' he prompted when she didn't go on.

'I saw the way you were ogling that actress's boobs. You do know they're fake, don't you?'

Jake could not believe what he was hearing. He

sincerely hoped it wasn't the sounds of jealousy. Because jealousy meant only one thing.

'I dare say it was the cameraman doing the ogling,' he said coldly. 'Not me.'

'That's not the way I saw it. Just remember that if you're dating me, Jake darling, you can look, but you can't touch anyone else.'

'Don't start getting possessive on me, Olivia,' he warned, his tone darkly ominous.

There was a short silence before she suddenly laughed. 'Of course not. I was only kidding. Any red-blooded man would have to be blind not to ogle Maddie Hanks's boobs. That's why they pay her so much to take off her clothes. So when am I going to see you next? I was thinking we could meet up somewhere in the city for dinner tomorrow night. Café Sydney, perhaps?'

Jake knew if he did that then Olivia would want to come back to his place for the night. And he simply didn't want to have sex with her. Truth be told, he'd been glad she'd gone away the previous weekend. After Craig's wretched funeral and wake he'd just wanted to be alone.

'I don't think so, Olivia,' he told her, trying not to sound as cold and hard as he suddenly felt towards her. But in his head he kept comparing her to Abby, who had cried in his arms over a man she hardly knew. And that was before she knew what he'd left her. Olivia might look all woman but she didn't have a soft or compassionate bone in her body. She could read the most tragic news and shed not a single tear.

'But why not?' Olivia demanded to know in the stroppy tone she adopted when things weren't going her way.

'I just don't feel like going out at the moment,' he replied wearily. 'I'm still down about Craig's death.'

'Then the best thing for you is to get out and about!'

'I said no, Olivia.'

'But I've missed you,' she went on, changing her tone to wheedling. 'Okay, how about I come to your place and we can get some food delivered?'

'Olivia, you're not hearing me. I don't feel like company at the moment. Please don't make a fuss. I'll ring you later in the week. We'll go out somewhere Saturday night.'

'Why not Friday night?'

'I've an early engagement Saturday morning.'

'Doing what?'

Jake sighed. He was an expert at picking up when his girlfriends started wanting more from him than what they'd agreed to. He sensed that something had changed over the weekend. Possibly something to do with this friend of hers getting married.

'Olivia, look, I...'

'Gosh, but don't you sound serious,' Olivia broke in, her voice light and teasing. 'I thought we promised each other never to get serious.'

'*You* were the one who was starting to sound serious,' Jake pointed out.

'Yes, I know. Silly me, getting all jealous about that actress. But you can't blame me, Jake. I'm competitive by nature and I just didn't like the way she looked at you. Like she was going to have you for supper.'

'Olivia, I have no intention of having anything further to do with Maddie Hanks. It was an interview. End of story.'

'Yes, of course. I'm sorry. Am I forgiven?'

What could he possibly say to that?

'Don't be angry with me, Jake,' she went on before he could find the right words.

'I'm not angry,' he said. Just dismayed.

'Excellent,' she said. 'Because I'm in desperate need of sex. And you, lover boy, are just the man to deliver.'

A week ago, before Craig's death, Jake would

have laughed. He'd always liked Olivia's slightly bawdy nature, plus her sometimes insatiable sex drive. Why, then, did he feel so disgruntled over her reducing him to the role of stud? He should have been pleased. And relieved. This was all he wanted from a woman, wasn't it?

An image suddenly popped into his mind, of another woman—one with lovely big eyes wet with tears—one who would never say things like that.

'I'm sorry, Olivia,' he said. 'But I'm not in the mood for sex right now.'

Her silence showed how much his rejection shocked her. Jake knew in his heart that this was the beginning of the end. Olivia was not going to be happy, but it was better to break up whilst they were still friends.

'Maybe you should find someone else,' he suggested quietly, hoping she would get the message without his having to spell it out.

'Like you have, you mean,' she threw at him. 'Who do you think you're kidding, Jake? You're always in the mood for sex. There's someone else, isn't there?'

Jake swallowed half a glass of wine before answering. 'No, Olivia,' he told her rather wearily.

'There's no one else.' It wasn't really a lie, even if Abby's face kept popping into his mind.

'Then who are you spending next Saturday morning with?' she demanded to know.

'If you must know, I'm taking Abby car shopping,' he said, well aware that it would cause trouble. But he no longer cared. He wanted Olivia out of his life.

'Abby who?' she screeched.

'Abby Jenkins,' he told her quite calmly. 'My housekeeper. Craig left me instructions in his will to buy her a car.'

'But…but…why would he do that?'

'Apparently she was nice to him when he stayed here a while back.'

'Nice to him in what way?' she said nastily.

How predictable she was. 'In her usual sweet way, I would imagine. Abby is a sweet girl.'

'*Girl!* I thought you said your housekeeper was a widow.'

'She is. Her husband died young.'

'I see. So how old is she, if I might ask?'

'Twenty-seven.'

'You never told me she was that young,' Olivia said, her tone accusing.

'Well, I'm telling you now.'

'Is she attractive?' she snapped.

'Olivia, I don't like the way this conversation is going.'

'Just answer the bloody question.'

'Abby's a very attractive girl.'

'I'll just bet she is. I dare say you wouldn't hire any other kind. So how long have you been sleeping with her?'

'I am not sleeping with her,' Jake denied. 'I hardly ever talk to her.'

'I don't believe you.'

Jake remained silent as his temper rose. If he spoke now, he'd say something he'd regret.

'You're not fooling me, Jake. You are sleeping with your housekeeper and nothing you say will make me believe otherwise.'

'In that case, I think we should call it quits, don't you?'

'Absolutely,' she said, and cut him off without another word.

Jake sighed. He preferred his relationships to end a little more civilly, and a lot more classily. But sometimes it just wasn't possible. A pity, though. Olivia had suited his lifestyle very well. Or she had, till Craig died and forced Jake to face what he had been secretly wanting for a long time: Abby.

No doubt Olivia would spread it around that

she'd come home from her weekend away to discover that Jake was sleeping with his house-keeper. He could deny it, of course. But he'd always found that denial fuelled rumours to greater heights. It wasn't as though any of this would reach Abby's ears. If he ignored the whispers around the channel—the TV world had a gossip grapevine second to none—by next week it would be yesterday's news.

Meanwhile, he had a week of shows to do and a difficult Saturday to endure.

Shoving his phone into his pocket, he stood up and made his way to the kitchen to make himself some supper before retiring for the night. As he extracted two slices of raisin bread from the freezer then popped them in the toaster, his thoughts slid back to Olivia's accusation that he was sleeping with Abby.

He wished!

Okay, so he possibly could seduce Abby if he put his mind to it. Jake knew he hadn't exactly been Prince Charming around her up till now. But seducing a woman like Abby would be a double-edged sword. Because she was the kind of woman men fell in love with—the kind of woman who made men want to marry them. Maybe even have children with them.

His mind boggled at this last thought!

Nope. Seducing Abby was one big no-no in Jake's head.

Now, if only he could convince his body to agree with him...

The toast popped up but Jake didn't notice. He was remembering how Abby's breasts had felt pressed hard against his chest. They were full and feminine and very soft. He wondered what kind of nipples she had. Would they be small and pink, or large and dusky? He didn't mind either way, as long as they were responsive.

Jake sucked in sharply once he realised where his thoughts were taking him.

'This is not good,' Jake muttered as he turned his attention to the rapidly cooling toast. He didn't want to be tempted to seduce Abby. It was a powerful temptation, though a dangerous one. Because, even if he managed to keep it to just an affair and not let his emotions get involved, Jake knew Abby didn't have the experience to handle an affair with a man like him. In the end, he would break her heart.

And it wasn't a hard-boiled heart like Olivia's. Abby's heart was soft and sweet. To risk breaking such a heart would be wicked. And Jake wasn't wicked. At the same time, he wasn't a saint. Best to keep physical contact with Abby to a minimum, came his firm lecture to himself. Be especially careful when you take her to that cemetery on Saturday, for starters. Whisk her away before she starts crying again. No more hugging. And not too much chit-chat.

Jake supposed he couldn't get out of helping her buy a new car, since she'd want to trade in that old ute and was sure to be taken advantage of by some slick salesman. But once he knew what kind of car she liked, he'd do a lot of the groundwork over the phone before Saturday then direct her straight to his chosen dealer, who would have her choice all registered and ready to go. That way there would be no dithering around. Before you could say Jack Robinson, she'd be driving off home in her new car, leaving him to watch her go with a clear conscience.

Humph! And who was he kidding? Jake suspected that by the end of Saturday his conscience—as well as his male hormones—would have been sorely tried. Hopefully, he would win the battle and not do anything stupid!

Crunching into a piece of cold raisin toast, he ripped off a large mouthful with a savagery which matched his mood. Jake hadn't felt this frustrated since he'd been laid up in hospital with a useless leg.

Life as a confirmed bachelor, he decided, wasn't all it was cracked up to be!

CHAPTER SEVEN

AFTER AN UNCHARACTERISTICALLY restless night, Abby woke with butterflies in her stomach. She didn't want to care what Jake might have done with that actress the night before. She didn't want to rush into the master bedroom as soon as she arrived at his house this morning. She certainly didn't want to be compelled to inspect the bed for evidence of a female visitor the night before.

But Abby knew that was exactly what she was going to do.

There was no use pretending differently. Her curiosity had been aroused by Megan's insistence that Jake would not be able to resist Maddie Hanks. It was all she'd thought about the evening before. She'd tried to read. She was on to the last of the list of ten books Craig had given her, Daphne du Maurier's *Rebecca*, which she was thoroughly enjoying. But even that hadn't distracted her from thinking about what Jake might be up to. She'd tossed and turned until well after midnight.

Strangely, despite less sleep than usual, she didn't feel tired. Just annoyed. With herself. Even more so when she started dithering over what to wear to work.

'As if it matters what you look like,' she flung at herself, reaching for another pair of old jeans and an equally ancient T-shirt which had once been white and was now an unflattering shade of grey. 'He's not going to come home again while you're there today. Now stop all this nonsense about Jake Sanderson. Who he sleeps with is none of your business!'

Famous last words. For what did Abby do as soon as she let herself into his house? She dropped her bag in the hallway then dashed upstairs to the master bedroom, her heart going as fast as her feet.

It was a large room, dominated by a huge bed which could easily accommodate its long-limbed owner and whatever playmate—or playmates—he so desired.

Abby blinked.

Had Jake ever entertained more than one woman at a time in that bed?

It looked messy enough this morning to have

hosted a whole harem in there last night. Maybe he'd had the newsreader *and* the actress.

With some trepidation Abby approached the bed. Gingerly, she picked up one corner of the snow-white duvet and threw it back off the end of the bed. That was followed by the top sheet, revealing nothing but a rather crumpled bottom sheet. No female perfume wafted up to her nostrils, the only smell being Jake's, which was a mixture of man and the sandalwood scent belonging to his aftershave.

Still not certain that he hadn't had company, Abby bolted into the en suite bathroom to see how many towels had been used since yesterday. Only two, she noted, flung carelessly over the bath as was Jake's habit. If he'd had someone to stay then she hadn't showered in here, or used a fresh towel.

Abby let out a deep sigh of satisfaction.

'I told you he's not a sleazebag, Megan,' she said aloud.

Feeling much better, Abby went downstairs, collected her bag from the hallstand and made her way to the kitchen. There, she put on the kettle before proceeding into the utility room to inspect Jake's whiteboard, which was empty. She'd returned to the kitchen and just poured herself some coffee when her phone rang, her heart jumping when she saw the identity of her caller.

'Hello,' she said, unable to hide the surprise in her voice. 'What's up?'

'Nothing's up,' her boss answered after a moment's hesitation. 'I just wondered if you'd decided what kind of car you wanted yet. And what colour.'

'I... I haven't got around to that yet. Sorry,' she added.

'No need to apologise. But could you decide by tomorrow? That way I can have it ready for you by Saturday. Perhaps give me two choices of colours though, to be on the safe side. White is always a good pick. It's cooler and holds its value better.'

'Yes, yes, I know you're right. But I rather like blue.'

He sighed. 'What colour blue?'

'Not pale blue. Or turquoise. A royal blue.'

'Right. A royal blue. I know the Hyundai i30 comes in a nice royal blue. One of my assistants on the show has one and she loves it. Look, check it out on the internet and give me a ring tonight with your decision. Also, work out what bank account you want your money put into.'

'Okay,' she said, thinking to herself that he really was in a hurry to have done with all this, a thought which was a bit of a downer. It came to Abby that, against all logic and common sense, she was beginning to have feelings for Jake which were not only unwise but pointless.

It was all Megan's fault, she decided irritably, for putting silly ideas in her head.

'Make sure you have your old car looking as good as you can on Saturday so you can get the best trade-in possible.'

'Oh, but I'm not going to trade in the ute,' she told him. 'I'm going to give it to my sister. She doesn't have a car.'

'Right,' he said slowly.

'Is that a problem?'

'No, no, I suppose not.'

His attitude once again betrayed a degree of annoyance. No doubt he would prefer to spend this Saturday doing anything but chauffeuring her around to cemeteries and car yards. But really, there was no other solution if he wanted this all done and dusted as quickly as possible.

'Okay,' he went on after a longish hesitation. 'Ring me tonight and tell me if you're happy with that Hyundai and I'll get the ball rolling. But if they don't have any royal blues on the lot then it might have to be white.'

'That's all right. It doesn't really matter. What time should I ring?' She didn't want to ring him whilst he was out with his girlfriend. Or anyone else who would remain nameless.

'Any time after six. I'm not going out tonight.'

Why did she have to like the sound of that so much?

'Okay. Thanks, Jake. For everything.'

'No sweat. Bye.'

Abby just stood there for a while after they'd both clicked off, her head in a bit of a whirl. Pointless it might be, but she was definitely going to buy herself some new clothes before next Saturday. No way could she go car shopping with Jake looking anything but her best.

Thursday night was late-night shopping. Perhaps she would take Megan with her. Then again perhaps she wouldn't. Not only would her sister ask awkward questions about why she was buying new clothes all of a sudden, but Megan would also steer Abby into buying clothes which were to *her* taste, which meant tight and tarty.

Feminine pride demanded she look nice for Jake on Saturday, but not tarty.

No, she would go shopping by herself and buy

a few mix and match things which weren't too expensive but which fitted properly and made her feel good. She might also indulge herself with a trip to the hairdresser. Get her hair trimmed and a treatment put in. Maybe have her nails done at the same time.

No, not her nails. That was going too far. She didn't want Jake to think she was trying to doll herself up for him. She just wanted to look as good as she could. She'd felt ashamed of herself yesterday in those daggy old clothes with her hair scraped back and not a scrap of make-up on. If she was really going to move on with her life, it was high time she started looking after herself.

She'd really let herself go since Wayne died. Abby vowed she would turn over a new leaf tonight by having a long relaxing bath and giving her whole body some well needed attention.

Once she had a firm plan of action, Abby got started on the house. On Tuesday afternoons she always popped down to the supermarket to re-stock Jake's cupboards and fridge. When she'd started this job, Jake had given her a long list of food items that he didn't like to run out of.

He occasionally cooked meals for himself, though not often. Abby suspected he ordered takeaway a fair bit. Mostly Asian food. She'd seen the many and varied brochures on top of his fridge, plus the empty cartons in the bin. Abby had never seen the signs of a proper dinner party, despite the house having a lovely dining room with a beautiful big table and eight chairs. He probably took people out to dinner instead. Or maybe his current girlfriend gave dinner parties for him at her place.

Abby was wondering if this Olivia was as good a cook as *she* was, when she pulled herself up with a jolt.

You have to stop this, Abby Jenkins, she lectured herself. *Jake Sanderson is your boss and that's all he'll ever be. There is no point thinking about him, or his sex life, or what his girlfriends do or don't do. It's just as well you'll be leaving this job soon and going overseas before the man becomes some kind of sick obsession. You're lonely, that's all. So go get that shopping done then get yourself home, and around seven ring Jake and, for pity's sake, just keep the conversation businesslike.*

She wished she hadn't asked him to take her to the cemetery to visit his uncle's grave but it was too late now. He'd think she was loopy if she kept changing her mind. She'd just have to be careful not to cry. Because she didn't want him hugging her again. Gracious, no. No more hugging!

By the time Abby arrived home, a degree of depression had taken hold, this sudden unexpected attraction towards Jake making her acutely aware of just how lonely her life was. Really, she had no close friends other than her sister. Most of her neighbours worked in the city and were gone all day. Then at the weekends their lives were taken up with their children and their houses. Occasionally she was invited to a barbecue, but not often.

There was only one neighbour she would classify as a friend, an elderly widow who'd been very kind to her when Wayne died, but who, unfortunately, was also a terrible gossip. Abby hadn't told Harriet that her boss was the celebrity host of *Australia at Noon*, knowing that if she let that little gem drop she would be bombarded with questions about Jake. She'd just said her boss was called Mr Sanderson—which was a common enough name—and was a bachelor businessman who worked long hours in the city and needed someone to look after the house for him. When Harriet assumed he was a middle-aged workaholic who was married to his job, Abby let her.

Abby had been relieved to see that her next-door neighbour Harriet's car wasn't in her driveway, which meant she was out and therefore wouldn't be dropping in for a cuppa as she sometimes did when Abby arrived home from work. Abby wasn't in the mood for gossip.

There was no doubt that life hadn't been very kind to her. Firstly there was her teeth, which had been a huge problem in her eyes but which her parents had dismissed as nothing. Probably because it would have cost money to fix and they'd spent all their spare cash on alcohol. Then, shortly after her father had been killed in a drunken pub brawl, her mother had also died, succumbing to too many sleeping tablets downed with too much gin.

The coroner had called it an accidental death as opposed to suicide, but what did it really matter in the end? There'd been no life insurance to consider.

Abby had only been seventeen at the time, just entering her last year in high school. It had been impossible to do well at her studies while living in a refuge. She'd left school in the end to work full-time at the local fish and chip shop, earning enough by working seven days a week to rent the small flat above the shop for herself and Megan.

At twenty she'd married Wayne but she'd been unable to carry a baby full term.

That was the cruellest cut of all, even crueller, in a way, than Wayne's tragic drowning. Because, more than anything in the world, Abby wanted to have children, wanted to create a happy family, wanted to be the best mother in the world. Instead, she hadn't even had the chance.

When tears dripped from her nose into her tea, Abby shook her head quite violently, determined not to dwell on the past any more, or on anything negative.

'Time to run a bath and start looking after yourself, kiddo,' she said aloud, smiling at how much like Megan she sounded.

Her mood was still up when she picked up her phone to ring Jake at seven. Okay, so she found the man attractive. Most of the women in Australia did. There was no need to get into a twist over it. Nothing would come of it, and soon she'd be off overseas on the holiday of a lifetime.

Given all her common sense reasoning, it annoyed Abby that her hand still shook as she lifted her phone to her ear and waited for Jake to answer.

'Hi, Abby,' Jake answered in his usual businesslike voice. So why did the sound of it suddenly have her stomach curling over and her heart beating faster? 'Made up your mind about the car?'

In truth, Abby didn't really give a hoot about the make and model of the car. She was thrilled just to be getting a brand-new one. Not so thrilled that she was acting like some schoolgirl with a crush on her teacher.

'I like the look of that Hyundai you mentioned. And it doesn't have to be royal blue. A white one would be fine.'

'Good. I'll pick you up at ten on Saturday morning. Is that too early for you?'

'No, no. Ten will be fine.' She'd be ready at dawn if he wanted.

'See you Saturday morning.'

He was gone before she could say another word, leaving her with a dry mouth and the sure knowledge that the next few days were going to be the longest in her life.

CHAPTER EIGHT

BY FRIDAY JAKE found it difficult to concentrate on the preparations for his show. Or care. He hadn't been sleeping well and, quite frankly, doing this damned show every day was beginning to bore him silly.

There was no doubt now that he would sell it and do something else with his life, something more challenging, preferably overseas and well away from a certain girl who he couldn't get out of his mind. Instead of going over his notes for the show like he usually did, he kept thinking about tomorrow.

The door to his dressing room suddenly opened.

'Five minutes, Jake,' Kerrie said.

'Yeah, yeah, I'm ready.' Though he wasn't.

He did the show on autopilot that day, no one guessing that his mind was elsewhere. Or so he'd imagined. Afterwards, the director pulled him aside and asked him if there was anything wrong.

'No,' Jake said. 'Why?'

'A little birdie told me you've been having girl trouble.'

Jake smiled a wry smile. He'd known Olivia would become vicious and vengeful.

'Not me, Victor. I never have girl trouble.'

Victor didn't look convinced. 'Not telling, eh? Fair enough. But it's never wise to let your private life affect your professional life. The lights were on today, Jake, but nobody was home.'

Jake shrugged. 'Just a bit tired, that's all.'

'No sweat. No one else would have noticed. Only old eagle-eye here. But it might be an idea to get some shut-eye tonight. Man does not live by sex alone.'

Jake laughed drily. 'I wish.'

'So the rumours were right? Olivia's been dumped in favour of your sexy young house-keeper?'

Jake rolled his eyes. 'I didn't *dump* Olivia. We broke up because she jumped to the wrong conclusion about my housekeeper, who's a very nice, *sweet* girl and definitely *not* my lover.'

Again, Victor didn't look convinced.

When Jake's phone rang he stared at the identity of the caller, his emotions suddenly a-jangle. He hoped nothing had happened to prevent them getting together tomorrow. The truth was he couldn't wait to see her. 'I have to take this call,' he said sharply, then strode off down the corridor.

'Yes, Abby?' Jake said, an attack of anxiety making his stomach swirl. 'What is it?' He didn't mean to sound so abrupt but he was shocked by his nervous reaction to the possibility that he might not be seeing her the next day after all. 'I hope you're not going to change tomorrow's arrangements,' he snapped before he could stop himself.

'What? No, no. I just wanted to ask you if I could go home early today. I was going to do some late-night shopping last night but my sister wasn't well and she needed me to look after Timmy for her.'

Relief swamped Jake, as did remorse over his snapping at her like that.

'Of course you can go home early.'

'I've done everything I had to do.'

'I'm sure the place is perfect,' Jake said. 'It always is. What do you need to buy?' he added, hoping to redeem himself by showing an interest in her life for once.

'Just some new clothes so that I don't embarrass you tomorrow by looking like your cleaning lady. Even if I am,' she added with a sweet laugh.

'You are much more than my cleaning lady,' Jake said, the devil's voice whispering in his ear that he would like her to be a hell of a lot more. 'As I said the other day, you are the best house-keeper a man could have.'

Her sudden silence brought a tension to Jake which was wickedly sexual. Heat licked through his loins, giving him an inkling of how it would feel if she ever surrendered to him.

He had no idea what she was thinking but he hoped she might be softening towards him a lit-tle. Or was he just fantasising? Abby had been making him fantasise a lot lately, all of it rather R-rated. How many times this week had he pic-tured going home early and sweeping her up into his arms, kissing her senseless and having her then and there? His favourite fantasy scenario was to hoist her up on to the kitchen bench-top where he would spread her legs—she'd be some-how naked, of course—and sink into her as she wrapped her arms around his neck and urged him on and on. Then there was the polished floor scenario. And the one against the wall. In the lap pool. Across the dining table.

His raunchy fantasies were multiplying.

Deplorable, really.

And very dangerous.

Because they were oh, so exciting.

'So everything's still right for tomorrow?' he asked, his cool voice belying the heat in his body.

'What? Oh, yes…yes. I'll be ready. Ten o'clock, you said, didn't you?'

'Yes. Oh, and Abby, what account do you want the twenty-five thousand put into?'

'Just put it in the one my salary goes in.'

'Very well. I'll do that this afternoon.'

'I… I don't know what to say except thank you.'

'It's Craig you should be thanking.'

'I will, when I visit his grave tomorrow.'

'You do that. See you tomorrow then.'

'But you don't know my address.'

'Of course I do. It was on your CV, which is still in my computer. You haven't moved, have you?'

'No.'

'Then I'll see you at your place at ten on the dot. Have to go. Bye.'

Jake sighed heavily as he clicked off his phone.

It was always an intimate situation, driving a woman somewhere, especially in a car which had once been described by a motoring magazine as sex on wheels. Jake figured Abby had never seen his red Ferrari. During the week he kept it locked away in the garage. He always used the ferry to get to and from work, and took taxis if he was socialising in and around the city. The Ferrari was only brought out at weekends for drives either up or down the coast. Jake liked nothing better than to zoom along one of the freeways with the top down and a beautiful woman by his side, one who was as responsive as his car.

Jake suddenly recalled his thoughts the other day about Abby's breasts, and how responsive they might be. If he closed his eyes he could still feel how they had felt, pressed up against him.

He cursed and jumped to his feet. This was all getting beyond a joke. Anyone would think he didn't have any self-control. He needed to stop all this nonsense immediately and just act naturally with her. He would not, he resolved, do or say anything provocative or seductive or, God forbid, charming.

An affair with Abby was out of the question.

Still, as Jake headed out of the dressing room, he resolved not to tempt fate by putting the top down on the Ferrari on Saturday. Better to be safe than sorry.

CHAPTER NINE

FOR THE UMPTEENTH time that morning, Abby smiled at herself in her large bathroom mirror, which was, actually, the only mirror she had in her house. All those years of having horrible teeth had made her allergic to mirrors. She still wasn't entirely used to her new appearance. Still didn't smile as much as other people.

But Megan was right. Her face did look much better now that her teeth were lovely and even and white. Her face looked a lot better with some make-up on as well, and with her hair all shiny and blow-dried properly.

Deciding that she'd admired herself long enough, Abby returned to her bedroom, where she'd laid out all the clothes she'd bought after her trip to the hairdresser. Abby hadn't splurged out on too much—a couple of pairs of stretchy jeans and a few tops and T-shirts, all of them cheap but in fashion. She'd also bought a light-weight blazer, a pair of trendy sandals and a new handbag. Finally, she'd splurged on a delicate gold necklace which went with everything, along with some new make-up, nail polish and a small bottle of perfume.

All in all she'd only spent just over three hundred dollars, which she considered very reasonable. Really, you didn't have to spend a lot on clothes these days, and it was about time she made more of an effort with her appearance. With today promising to be warmer than yesterday, she selected the white jeans and a short-sleeved silky top that had a white background and little brown dots all over it. The slinky fabric hugged her curves and the scooped neckline was perfect for her new dainty gold chain.

A glance at the digital clock beside the bed made Abby sigh. Only nine o'clock, excitement having got her up at the crack of dawn. She had a whole hour before Jake was due to arrive. That was, if he even arrived on time. People didn't seem to care about punctuality these days. She supposed it would take her a while to do her nails, but not an hour.

As the minutes ticked slowly away she became aware of her heart beating faster behind her ribs. Beside the excitement of a new car, she was nervous at the thought of being with Jake outside of a work environment. Would he think she looked pretty in her new clothes? Did she want him to think her pretty? Did she want him to...what?

Abby knew she was being foolish. He had a girlfriend. A gorgeous girlfriend. Why would he look at her twice? Why would she even want him to?

He's your boss, she reminded herself firmly. *And he's only doing all this because his uncle asked him to. He doesn't want to spend time with you. He doesn't want to buy you a new car or take you to a cemetery. Not really. He's honouring his beloved uncle's deathbed wishes. Get a grip, girl.*

The sight of a bright red sports car careering down her street was not a sight designed to make a girl get a grip.

Abby wasn't surprised when the sleek red car with the prancing horse logo on it slid into the kerb outside her house. For who else would drive a Ferrari but a man who'd been voted not only the most popular television personality but also Sydney's most eligible bachelor?

Megan kept her well informed about all aspects of her boss's professional and private life.

'Oh, *my,*' Abby murmured when Jake emerged from the driver's side, looking even sexier than his car, if that were possible. Up till now Abby had only ever seen her boss dressed in a business suit. Today, he was wearing a pair of chinos and a black polo shirt which hugged the contours of his upper body, showing off his naturally broad shoulders and nicely flat stomach. As he strode around the low-slung bonnet of the car, a lock of his dark brown hair fell across his forehead. Jake lifted his hand and impatiently combed it back with his fingers. The action brought Abby's attention to his face. It wasn't the face of a pretty boy but very handsome all the same, with a strong straight nose and a ruggedly squared jawline. His blue eyes—possibly his best feature—were hidden by a pair of expensive-looking sunglasses.

For a split second, Abby wondered what her neighbours would think when Jake walked up to her front door. It was a lovely spring day so quite a few of them were out in their gardens, mowing lawns and tending to their flowerbeds. Not that they would recognise him. He could be anyone in those glasses. Anyone handsome and very rich, that was.

Abby took a backwards step from the window when Jake stopped on the pavement to stare at her house, her hackles rising as he continued to stare at it for some time. What was he staring at? she wondered.

Abby wasn't in any way ashamed of her home. Okay, so it was small and old, built not long after the war. But it was nicely painted and neat, with well kept gardens, front and back. Inside, each of the rooms was equally well painted, the wooden floors shiny and polished. The furniture *was* on the cheap side but it had been bought new and looked quite stylish, like the clothes she was wearing.

He finally opened the gate and strode up the path to the small front porch, Abby using those few precious seconds to get a handle on her suddenly defensive mood.

It wasn't like her to be sensitive about criticism; it was a survival habit she'd acquired over her school years when her supposed friends had made bitchy comments about her teeth. But Abby suspected she would be very hurt if Jake made her feel small, especially today when she felt so good about herself. Hopefully, he wouldn't. He didn't seem an unkind person. But then, she didn't really know him all that well, did she?

The doorbell ringing made her heart jump,

then race like mad. Lord, but she was getting herself into a right state. Gathering herself, Abby hurried to the front door, her head held high.

CHAPTER TEN

JAKE THOUGHT HE'D steeled himself sufficiently by the time he'd rung the doorbell, having given himself a firm lecture during the drive over. He'd told himself in no uncertain terms that he had to stop fantasising about what Abby might be like in bed and concentrate on the job his uncle had entrusted him with.

Craig certainly hadn't included seduction in his dying wishes.

Even after he'd arrived, Jake had lingered outside for another minute or so, harnessing all his willpower for the mental and physical battle he had ahead of him.

Jake thought he was well prepared until Abby opened the door.

His startled gaze raked over her from top to toe before returning to her face. He'd found her attractive before. Today she looked downright stunning, and so desirable it was criminal.

Thank goodness he was wearing sunglasses, the kind you couldn't see through.

What to say? Nothing personal. Nothing too complimentary. She might think he was coming on to her.

'Don't you look nice,' he said.

If only she hadn't smiled at him. Such a beautiful smile.

'I went on a bit of a shopping splurge last night,' she said a little sheepishly. 'I hope Craig would approve. I didn't spend too much.'

'I'm sure he wouldn't mind,' Jake said. But *he* did. That outfit she had on was extremely sexy, those tight white jeans contrasting with the silky top which skimmed her hips and left her full breasts oh, so accessible. In his mind's eye, Jake immediately saw himself pressed up behind her, their lower halves glued together whilst his hands slid up underneath, cupping her breasts. In his fantasy she moaned softly, her head tipping back against his shoulder. She moaned again when he unclipped her bra and took her erect nipples between his thumbs and forefingers and squeezed them.

Hard.

It was impossible to think such wickedly erotic thoughts and not have his body respond.

Alarmed that Abby might notice, Jake did the only thing he could think of.

'Would you mind if I used your bathroom before we get going?' he asked with some urgency.

'It's the second door on the right,' Abby directed him.

Abby smiled as she watched Jake head for the bathroom, thrilled to pieces with his compliment on her appearance. And whilst she was flattered and pleased—she was a female after all—she was quite confident that Jake was not about to pounce on her the way Megan had said he might. She'd sent her sister pictures of her new clothes last night, and been subjected to renewed warnings over the male species and their lack of conscience and morals where pretty girls were concerned.

'Playboys like your Jake are the worst,' Megan had pointed out. 'They think they can't be resisted and, unfortunately, that's often true. Hard to resist a good-looking man with charm and money.'

When Abby argued that she'd never found Jake all that charming, Megan had just laughed.

'That's because you haven't been a target before. Once he gets a look at you in your new things he'll go into charm mode in no time flat. First will come the compliments, then the accidental touches, followed by flirtatious remarks, finishing up with a drinks or dinner invitation. You mark my words, kiddo.'

At this point, Abby had decided not to tell Megan that *she* would be the one extending a dinner invitation. As a thank you gesture. Truly, sometimes it was best not to tell Megan things.

Still, she had to confess that she'd got a real buzz when he'd said how nice she looked.

Whilst Jake was in the bathroom, Abby collected her new bag from the lounge, then picked up the house keys from the hall table so she'd be ready to lock up when Jake was finished. She understood that he didn't want to waste the whole of his precious Saturday with her when he could be with his girlfriend. His attitude to this whole business had been one of impatience from the start.

Jake took his time, however, Abby's gaze travelling back to his car whilst she waited.

Now that was another thing she'd definitely not be telling Megan. Abby hadn't known till today what kind of car Jake drove so she would invent a nice safe sedan, if need be. She could just imagine what Megan would say if she found out her sister had spent Saturday afternoon swanning around in Jake's sexy red Ferrari.

By the time Jake left the bathroom he'd gathered himself, ready to face his tormentor with his body almost under control and his sunglasses firmly in place.

Jake wondered again what was making her so irresistible to him. Was it her relative innocence? Her lack of experience?

It wasn't just her beauty. He'd had lots of beautiful women in his life, and in his bed. No, it was something else. Something intangible. Something very sweet and very special.

It made him afraid for her.

He'd been right to be fearful, he decided as he watched Abby turn to lock up, her rear view as tasty as her front. He suppressed a groan and willed his own body to behave.

It ignored him and Jake swore at himself in his head.

'How long will it take to get to the cemetery?' she asked innocently as she turned back to face him.

'Not long,' he said a bit abruptly. 'I've also already contacted the dealership in Parramatta,' he went on, masking his inner torment behind his best businesslike voice. 'I spoke to a salesman there at length yesterday and they have a car on their lot which should suit you admirably. If you like it, you could drive it away today. It's all registered and ready to go.'

'Really?' She sounded pleased. 'What colour is it?'

'White. Sorry. No blue ones available. But really, it's the most sensible colour for our climate and city. Never gets too hot or looks too dirty.'

She laughed, bringing a sparkle to her eyes and some added colour to her cheeks. She was making things awfully hard for him.

And wasn't that an understatement? came the wry thought. Thank goodness he wasn't wearing tight jeans.

'I can't imagine me ever letting any car of mine get too dirty,' she said, 'especially a new one. Megan calls me a neat freak.'

'A good quality in a housekeeper,' he said through gritted teeth. And in a lover, came the pesky thought.

Jake liked his women well groomed. All over. Liked their clothes to be just so, especially their underwear. When he started wondering what Abby had on underneath that top and jeans he knew it was time to get this show on the road. 'Come on, let's get going.'

Quite automatically, he went to reach out and take her elbow, a habit he had when escorting a woman. He pulled his hand back just in time, instead waving her on ahead of him.

Damn, he thought wearily as he trudged after her. It was going to be a long morning.

CHAPTER ELEVEN

A VERY HAPPY Abby was striding along her front path towards the gate when Harriet, her elderly neighbour, suddenly popped her head up over the hedge which separated their two houses.

'Hello, dear,' she said. 'My, but don't you look extra nice today. Going somewhere special?' Her curious eyes zoomed from Abby to Jake to the Ferrari then back to Abby again.

Abby suppressed a sigh as she reluctantly ground to a halt and turned towards her neighbour. 'Just going car shopping,' she replied truthfully. 'Got a windfall from a long-lost uncle. My friend here's going to help me find the right one,' she said, casting a rueful glance over her shoulder at Jake. 'He's a car nut, as you can see. Can't stop and chat,' she hurried on, not wanting to have to get into awkward introductions.

'We're already running late,' she added, and headed for the Ferrari. 'Bye.'

'Drop in for a cuppa tomorrow,' Harriet called after her.

'Will do,' she called back.

Jake didn't say a word as he swiftly opened the passenger door for her. Neither did he help her, despite it not being the easiest car to get into. But Abby had always been an agile sort of girl, with long slender legs and sure hands, so by the time Jake closed the door and walked around to the driver's side she was all buckled up and ready to go, her new handbag settled in her lap.

'A car nut, am I?' Jake said wryly after he climbed in and gunned the engine.

Abby shrugged. 'I had to say something.'

'Will you really go in for a cuppa tomorrow?' he asked as he accelerated away.

'Probably,' Abby admitted. 'Harriet was very good to me when Wayne died. I wouldn't hurt her for the world. I just didn't want to have to introduce you.'

'Why's that?'

'Well, mostly because I don't want her to find out that you're the businessman I clean house for. She'd immediately think that there was something going on between us and, before I knew it, the whole street would think the same thing, which would be very embarrassing. Gosh, but this car is amazing,' she rattled on, happy to change the subject from their hypothetical affair. 'It must have cost you a small fortune.'

'There are more expensive cars but it wasn't cheap. I only drive it at weekends and when I'm on holiday.'

'It's not a convertible though, is it?'

'Actually, it is. The top retracts.'

'That's incredible!'

He said nothing for a few seconds, though he did glance over at her with a bit of a frown. But then he smiled a strange little smile as though he was secretly amused about something.

'I'll show you, if you like,' he said.

His offer startled her. 'Oh, no. No, please don't. Not today. My hair will get all messed up and it took me ages to do it.'

'Fair enough. Some other time then.' And he smiled another strange smile.

Abby could not envisage there would ever be such a time, which was a shame really. It would be wonderful whizzing along an open country road on a fine summer's day with the top down and her hair blowing in the breeze. Even better if she were driving.

She almost laughed. Imagine her driving a Ferrari. She wasn't a Ferrari kind of girl.

Jake was right. The cemetery wasn't far away but it was a depressing place. Abby didn't like the long rows of gravestones.

She hadn't buried Wayne. He'd been cremated with his ashes sprinkled in the ocean at his favourite fishing spot. Which was ironic given it was the sea which had killed him. But it was what he had once told her he wanted, if anything ever happened to him. Perhaps, however, he'd imagined being killed in a car accident, not what had actually happened.

'This way,' Jake said after they both climbed out. He set off at a brisk walk, not looking back to see if she was behind him. Which was so typical of her boss.

No charm yet, Megan, she said silently to her sister. One little compliment was as much as he could manage.

Abby followed Jake down a long row of well tended graves, some of which had fresh flowers in vases on them. She hadn't thought to bring flowers, her mind being on nothing but looking her very best this morning, a realisation which upset her a little. Stupid, Abby. Get your priorities straight!

Still, Jake might have thought it was overdoing things if she'd brought flowers.

He stopped suddenly in front of a freshly dug grave which was covered with a large green felt blanket topped with a huge arrangement of native flowers which didn't look at all bedraggled, although they had to have been there over a week.

'That's Craig's grave,' he pointed out, his rough voice betraying a depth of emotion which moved Abby.

Clearly, he had loved his uncle. A lot. Craig's death must have upset Jake terribly, his grief heightened by not having been able to be with the man when he'd died. It had been a cruel thing for his uncle to do. He'd probably thought he was being kind, and brave. But it had been selfish of him, really. Selfish and insensitive.

Abby opened her mouth to say something sympathetic, but when she looked up at Jake she found him staring down, not at his uncle's grave but at the grave on the left of it. The name on the gravestone was Clive Sanderson, beloved husband of Grace, much loved father of Roland, Peter, Jake, Sophie, Cleo and Fiona.

It didn't take a genius to realise this had to be Jake's father, the dates revealing he'd died at the age of forty-seven. How sad. What to say?

Nothing, Abby decided. She understood enough about her boss to know that he wouldn't want to talk about it. So she returned her attention to Craig's grave, closed her eyes and said a prayer of thanks to him, at the same time adding that he really should have told his family that he was dying.

But it was too late to change anything now, she accepted. Death was very final. It took no prisoners, as the saying went. When Abby felt tears prick at her eyes she blinked them away then looked over at Jake.

'I've said my thanks,' she said matter-of-factly. 'I think I'd like to go now.'

'Good,' he said, and stalked off in the direction of the car, not saying another word till they were both back in their seats. Only then did he speak.

'I'm sorry,' he apologised. 'I still can't get over his death.'

'Your uncle's, or your father's?' she asked gently.

'Ah. You saw.' He loosened his grip on the wheel and turned to face her. 'Both really. But Craig's is still very raw.'

'It gets easier with time,' was all she could offer. Though, down deep, Abby knew some deaths stayed with you for ever.

He sighed, leant back against the car seat, took

off his sunglasses then glanced over at her. 'How did your husband die, Abby?'

'He drowned,' came her rather stark reply. But there was little point in not telling him the truth. 'He went out fishing in a small dinghy not suitable for the open sea. A storm came up and he was tipped into the water. He wasn't wearing a life belt. His body was washed up on Maroubra Beach a couple of days later.'

'You must have been devastated,' he said quietly, his eyes sad for her.

'I was.'

He nodded at the obvious sincerity in her statement. 'You are a lovely young woman,' he went on with a sigh. 'You'll find someone else eventually, get married again and have lots of equally lovely children.'

She laughed. She couldn't help it. 'I don't think so, Jake. I don't want to get married again.'

'You loved him that much?'

It was one thing to tell her boss the brutal truth about Wayne's death, but everything else was her own private business. She would not share it with him.

'It's not a question of love, Jake, but what I want to do with the rest of my life. I thought I wanted marriage and children when I was younger, but my priorities have changed. I want to travel whilst I'm still young. I want to see another side of life than just what's here in Australia. I want to see the world.'

He looked over at her for a long time. 'I see,' he said at last.

Probably not, she thought.

'We'd better get going again,' he went on gruffly. 'We have a car to buy.'

CHAPTER TWELVE

'OH, JAKE, I simply adore it!' Abby exclaimed when she climbed in behind the wheel of the sporty white hatchback. 'Thank you so much.'

Jake just smiled and let the salesman, Raoul, continue showing Abby all the features of her new car. After he'd run through everything, Raoul suggested Abby take it for a test spin round the block. Jake declined her invitation to accompany her, which in hindsight was not a good move, since Raoul was only too happy to go in his place. The salesman was about Abby's age, an immigrant from South America, tall, dark and handsome with a sexy accent and charm by the bucketload. Jake wished within seconds of them disappearing down the street that he'd gone with Abby.

He was damned if he did and damned if he didn't! When she'd confessed her wish to spurn marriage and see the world, he'd been momentarily overcome with joy that now he could seduce her and not feel guilty about it. But Jake knew in his heart of hearts that a girl like Abby would want marriage and children again one day. And then there was the unpalatable added fact that whilst she was grateful to him, she clearly wasn't at all enamoured with his character.

Was it too late to turn on the charm?

He rather suspected that it was.

Jake paced the car lot until Abby returned, doing his best to calm down whilst inside he was churning with regret and, yes, jealousy, an emotion he despised. But it was no use. He was jealous. As soon as the white hatchback turned into the driveway he strode towards it, anxiously searching for evidence that the couple inside were in any way attracted to each other.

Raoul, it seemed, was doing all the talking whilst Abby was just nodding. When Abby climbed out and smiled over at *him*, Jake was so relieved that he smiled back.

'So how was it?' he asked as she walked towards him.

'Brilliant!' she exclaimed. 'And so easy to drive.'

'It certainly is,' Raoul said on joining them. 'But then, you are also a very good driver, Abby.'

She smiled over at him.

Jake's gut tightened. He didn't want her smiling at other men, especially this one. What was the point in controlling his own desire for the girl if she fell into the clutches of some slick-talking salesman?

Jake decided it was time to go.

'You're happy with that particular car then, Abby?' he directed at her.

'Oh, yes. Very happy.'

'Then we'll take it,' he told Raoul. 'I presume I can pay for it with my credit card.'

'But of course, Mr Sanderson. Come with me into my office and I'll fix up everything for you.'

'Lucky you,' Raoul said when he finally handed over the registration papers and keys, 'to have such a generous employer as Mr Sanderson.'

'He's a wonderful boss,' Abby agreed.

Jake winced inside. He'd explained to Raoul on the phone yesterday that Abby was a valued employee of his and the car was her Christmas bonus. Jake had informed Abby of his little white lie just before they'd arrived at the dealership, but he'd forgotten that the male mind often thought the worst when it came to an attractive female. Clearly, Raoul had jumped to the conclusion that Abby was getting this car as payment for services rendered outside work hours. Fortunately, Abby didn't seem aware of this. He just hoped that he could get her out of here before she twigged to the situation.

'Thank you for your assistance,' Jake said, standing up and extending his hand over the desk.

The salesman stood up and took his hand. 'My pleasure, Mr Sanderson,' he returned in a rather unctuous manner.

'Now, if you have any trouble, Abby,' Raoul went on, smiling over at Abby, who had also risen to her feet, 'any trouble at all, you just ring me. Here's my card.'

Abby took it, of course. Which irked Jake considerably. Couldn't she see he just wanted to get into her pants? Surely she wasn't *that* naïve?

'If you have any trouble with your car, Abby,' Jake bit out as he walked her over to it, 'you ring me first, not that sleazebag.'

Abby lifted startled eyes to his. 'You think Raoul's a sleazebag?'

'Yes, I do.'

Takes one to know one, Jake, came the brutally honest thought.

Abby's face fell. 'And there I was, thinking he

was just being extra nice. Because of you being famous, you know?'

Jake could see he'd upset her, which was the last thing he'd wanted to do. He'd loved seeing her so happy about the car.

'You could be right,' he said. 'Take no notice of me, Abby. I'm a cynical bastard at times.'

Abby frowned. 'No, you're probably right. Megan says I'm too trusting where men are concerned.' She glanced up at him and smiled. 'But I know a truly good one when I meet him. Which reminds me. I want to do something special for you, Jake, to thank you for everything.'

Jake tried not to let his mind trail over all the things he'd like her to do for him. But it went there all the same. She'd called him 'truly good', but he wasn't. Not at all.

He swallowed before he spoke, lest a thickened voice betray him. 'You don't have to do anything, Abby. It was my pleasure to follow through with Craig's wishes. He obviously liked and admired you a lot.'

She flushed prettily. 'Not as much as he liked and admired you. Look, I thought that perhaps I could cook you dinner one night. I know that's not much in the way of a thank you present, but I'm actually a very good cook.'

'I'm sure you are, Abby, but truly, it's not necessary.'

Her face fell again, which made him feel dreadful. After all, she didn't know the battle that was going on inside him. It was obvious she wanted to do this. A thought suddenly occurred which would hopefully save his sanity.

'Very well,' he agreed. 'Dinner it is. But not just for me,' he added. 'For my sister as well.'

Abby blinked her confusion. 'Your sister?'

'Yeah, my sister, Sophie. I promised to take her out to dinner next Friday night. She's the only one in my family who knows about Craig's letter and she was saying the other day that she'd love to meet you. We could kill two birds with one stone. What do you say, Abby? Would you mind cooking for her as well?'

'I wouldn't mind at all. But maybe your sister would mind.'

'Good heavens, no. She'd love it.'

'Well, if you're sure...'

'I'm very sure.'

'Your place or mine?'

Jake almost choked on the spot. 'What?'

'Do you want me to cook the dinner at my place or yours?'

What *had* he been thinking? About sex, of course. What else?

'I don't mind either way, Abby, but then I don't have a problem with neighbours. Perhaps we should have this dinner at my place?'

'Yes, I think that would be best.'

He looked at her and thought none of this was for the best. But Sophie's presence would at least stop him from doing something stupid—like piling on the charm and plying Abby with wine before carrying her up to bed and having his wicked way with her all night long.

'I presume you'll be okay to drive home alone in your new car,' he said. 'You won't be nervous, will you?'

'Maybe a little. But only because it's new. I really am a good driver. And the car has GPS. Even if it didn't, I know the roads around here like the back of my hand. I used to live out this way. The fish and chip shop I worked in for years is just around the corner.'

Jake was suddenly overwhelmed with curiosity about her life before coming to work for him, especially about her marriage and, yes, her drowned husband. The temptation to invite her to go for coffee with him somewhere was acute, but he resisted it.

Just.

'In that case I won't worry about you,' he said instead. 'Off you go then.'

Abby sighed. 'What a shame. I would have *loved* another ride in that gorgeous car of yours.'

Don't say a single word, his conscience insisted firmly.

Suddenly, Abby beamed up at him. 'But I'm going to enjoy driving my own gorgeous little car even more. Bye, Jake. And thanks again.'

'My pleasure,' he returned. And, despite everything else, it had been. How perverse was that?

He shook his head as he watched her drive off with surprising confidence, not hesitating before joining the traffic and changing lanes quite assertively. Naïve and vulnerable Abby might be in some ways, but in practical life skills she seemed experienced and assured.

Once again, he wondered about her life before she'd been widowed, and even before that. What kind of child had she been? What were her parents like? Had she been good at school? Possibly not, if she'd ended up working in a fish and chip shop. But she certainly wasn't dumb. When Raoul had been showing her all the features of the car, she'd been very quick on the uptake. She also claimed to be a good cook and Jake came to the conclusion that Abby would be good at anything she set her mind to.

Inevitably, his own mind shifted to other areas at which Abby might excel. She'd been married for quite a few years, after all. And she hadn't gone to work during all that time. Clearly, she'd been content to stay home and be the kind of old-fashioned housewife a lot of men craved, always being there when hubby came home. He could see her now, waiting on the man she loved hand and foot, giving him everything he desired, in bed and out. As much as Jake didn't want that kind of life—or wife—for himself, he could see its appeal. He could see Abby's appeal. He could feel it, right now. He didn't want to marry her, but he did want her.

'Damn and blast,' Jake growled to himself as he marched off to where he'd parked his own car. He virtually threw himself behind the wheel, slamming it with both fists in a burst of frustration unlike any he'd ever felt before.

When he eventually calmed down, he just sat there, thinking.

Jake decided he should never have broken up with Olivia. He wasn't the sort of man who liked to sleep alone for too long. And she would be a good distraction from Abby. But there was no going back now. And if he was honest he didn't really want to.

Maybe he should give Maddie Hanks a call. She was still in Sydney, he knew. Okay, so her charms were rather obvious but, on the plus side, she wasn't interested in becoming Mrs Jake Sanderson. She just wanted some fun and games whilst she was here. A man would have to be a fool to knock that back, especially one who was climbing the walls with frustration. She'd given him her number after the show and he'd politely put it in his phone, even though at the time he'd had no intention of acting on her none too subtle invitation.

But lots of water had gone under the bridge since then.

Jake pulled out his phone and brought up her number, his lips pursing as his finger hovered. Did he really want to go to bed with someone like that?

Jake could not believe it when he abruptly deleted Maddie Hanks's number and rang his sister instead.

Sophie answered quickly. 'Hi, Jake, darling. How are you bearing up? You know, I watched you yesterday on that silly show you do, and I thought you looked a bit down.'

'What do you mean, calling my show silly?'

'Perhaps silly is not the right word. Light-weight, then.'

'Still, hardly a compliment.' But she was right. It was lightweight. No wonder he was bored. He'd meant it to be a hard-hitting current affairs show when he'd conceived it, but it hadn't turned out that way.

'If the cap fits, wear it, Jake. Now, to what do I owe the pleasure of this call? You're not going to call off our dinner date next Friday, are you?'

'Not at all. But I have a favour to ask you...'

And he told her everything.

CHAPTER THIRTEEN

ABBY FELT SATISFIED as she surveyed the dinner table in Jake's formal dining room. She had copied the exquisite setting from one of her sister's magazines, having known straight away it would suit the polished wooden floors and white walls of Jake's dining room. She'd used Jake's cutlery and glassware, but she'd bought the snow-white tablecloth and white napkins, along with the red and black table mats and matching coasters from the magazine, which Abby had found in a city store.

Since Jake's dining table could seat eight she'd only set one end of it, with Jake at the head, his sister to his right and herself to his left. That way she was nearer the door and the kitchen. Abby had also bought a crystal candlestick as a centrepiece, which held one red candle. A vase of fresh flowers from her own garden sat on the carved wooden sideboard, along with a vanilla-scented candle which she hoped would mask any smell which might waft from the kitchen once she started cooking the prawns and scallops.

It had taken ages for Abby to settle on a menu for the dinner party. She didn't want to be dashing in and out to the kitchen all the time but, having been reassured by Jake over the phone that neither he nor Sophie were fussy eaters, she'd chosen a seafood platter entrée, rack of lamb for the main and a passionfruit-topped cheesecake which she'd cooked in advance and which she knew from experience tasted better after spending a day in the fridge. The various wines had come courtesy of recommendations from the man who owned her local wine shop.

A quick glance at her watch warned her that she only had twelve minutes before Jake and Sophie were due to arrive. Abby had told Jake over the phone that she didn't want him around whilst she was cooking, which hadn't seemed to bother him. Jake had said he'd go to his sister's place after work and they would drive to Balmain together.

Abby had had another reason for wanting Jake to be absent during her preparations for the evening. She'd wanted to surprise him with the table setting, not to mention the fact she was actually wearing a dress. When Jake had let slip that his sister was a professional stylist, Abby had gone shopping again, knowing instinctively that jeans were not the right sort of thing to wear for the dinner.

She did feel some guilt that she'd gone and bought some more clothes, but there was no denying the pleasure she got every time she looked at herself in the large mirror in Jake's hallway, which was what she was doing at this very moment, staring at herself and hoping Jake would like what he saw.

In one way, Abby wished it was just the two of them tonight. Though, really, that was all so much pie in the sky, hoping that he would suddenly fancy her the way Megan said he would. Abby knew how men acted when they fancied a woman and it certainly wasn't to organise a third person to be present when they could easily have been alone. On top of that, she wasn't at her best making conversation with strangers. And Jake's sister was a stranger.

No sooner had this wimpy thought entered Abby's head than it was banished.

'No more negative thoughts!' came her firm lecture as she stared at her reflection in the mirror and put on an assertive face. 'So you're a bit nervous about meeting Sophie. That's only

natural. She's a professional stylist—a sophis-
ticated career woman who's no doubt as good-
looking as her brother. But you'll be fine. You
look darned good yourself. And you're no dumb
blonde. You're smart. You know you are. Jake's
uncle thought so too.'

Whirling on her new high heels, Abby marched
back into the kitchen determined to be more confident.

'You're not very talkative,' Sophie said after
she parked her car outside Jake's place right on
seven. 'If I didn't know you better, I'd think you
were nervous.'

'Don't be ridiculous,' Jake snapped. 'I don't get
nervous.' Which was true. He was, however, ap-
prehensive about the evening ahead.

Despite having physically avoided Abby during the week, they'd talked a couple of times
over the phone. Nothing personal, just Abby
asking him about what foods he and his sister
liked. But even her voice did wicked things to
him. How was he going to cope with the real
thing tonight? During one phone call he'd been
so turned on, he'd been seriously tempted to tell
her Sophie couldn't make it and it would just be
the two of them.

If only Abby wasn't so darned sweet he might have done exactly that.

'Then what *is* your problem?' Sophie persisted as they walked up to the front door together. 'The girl said she didn't want to get married again. What's to stop you from dating her, if that's what you want?'

Jake threw his sister a convincingly exasperated look. 'Come on, sis. Abby only *thinks* she doesn't want marriage and children, but she'll change her mind about that eventually. Besides,' he added, 'she doesn't fancy me.'

Sophie laughed. 'Not only nervous but delusional. You've got it so bad your brain is addled. Of *course* she fancies you. That's why she offered to cook you dinner, you fool. You're not very good at reading between the lines, are you? And I thought you were a smart guy where women were concerned.'

'You don't understand,' Jake muttered as he inserted his key in the front door. 'I'm trying to do the right thing here.'

'Mmm… The road to hell is paved with good intentions, you know.'

'Yeah, I know. I'm already there.' And he pushed open the door.

'Something smells nice,' Sophie said on entering the hallway. 'Oh, look, it's a scented candle,' she added after peeking into the dining room. 'My, doesn't the table look lovely. Your Abby's gone to a *lot* of trouble.'

Jake heard the innuendo in Sophie's voice. 'Please don't start reading anything into this evening's dinner, sister dear. Abby has no romantic feelings for me whatsoever. She's just a very nice woman. This is gratitude, not lust.' *He* was the one in lust.

'Abby, we're here!' he called out as he took Sophie's arm and steered her down the hallway into the kitchen.

'My goodness!' he exclaimed. 'You're wearing a dress.' Or almost wearing one. His eyes clamped onto her cleavage and didn't budge.

Sophie winced at Jake's tone. Heavens, he made it sound as if wearing a dress was a crime.

Sophie watched the dismay on the girl's face quickly change to defiance.

'I am indeed,' she said as she came closer and twirled around for him to see her better.

Sophie tried not to smile at the look on her brother's face. Truly, the poor idiot was more than just smitten. If she didn't know him better, she might have thought he'd fallen in love. And she could see why.

Abby was one seriously attractive girl, with a delicately featured face with lovely greenish eyes, perfect skin and the most dazzling smile. There was nothing wrong with her figure either, which was most eye-catching, its hourglass shape shown to advantage in a floral wrap-around dress, the bodice crossing over her bust before tying into a bow on her left hip.

Of course, if Sophie had dressed her, she would have chosen a block colour rather than floral, and the V neckline would have been much lower. Why have great boobs if you didn't flaunt them, especially when you were young?

But all that was beside the point. The point at this precise moment was the way her brother was acting. Which was totally unacceptable.

Sophie decided to step in and smooth things over till Jake could get control of his hormones.

'I'm Sophie,' she introduced herself brightly, coming forward to give Abby a brief hug and a kiss on the cheek. 'That's a fab dress you're wearing. You'll have to tell me where you bought it. Did Jake mention that I'm in the fashion industry?'

Abby knew she would never give Sophie *that* information. The little black dress Jake's sister had on screamed luxury designer whereas

Abby's dress had been cheap as. But Sophie's kind compliments did make her feel better in the face of Jake's obvious disapproval. She did, however, feel somewhat comforted by the fact that Sophie wasn't drop dead gorgeous like her brother.

'Jake,' Sophie said sharply, 'stop glaring at Abby and tell her how lovely she looks.'

'She looks very nice,' he bit out. 'It was just a shock, that's all. I've never seen her in a dress before. How's the food going, Abby? I'm so hungry I could eat a horse.'

CHAPTER FOURTEEN

ABBY CONTROLLED HER temper with difficulty. 'Sorry. Horse isn't on the menu for tonight. You'll have to make do with lamb. Now, if you'd like to follow me into the dining room, I'll show you where you're both sitting.'

Jake winced when she swept past him with a hurt look cast his way. He knew he was behaving badly but he couldn't seem to find that much vaunted charm he was famous for. His social skills had completely deserted him in the face of a sexual attraction which was as cruel as it was powerful. Thank heavens he'd put his suit jacket back on before leaving Sophie's place. And thank heavens he would soon be sitting down.

Sophie came to his rescue, saying all the right things about the table setting, plus Abby's choice of wine. Jake finally opened his mouth to agree with his sister about the wine, which brought another cool look from Abby.

He fancied her even more when she was like this!

Jake tried not to stare when she poured Sophie some wine, but the action required her to bend forward, making the neckline of her dress gape a little. When she moved around to pour his wine, he kept his eyes firmly on the tablecloth. He knew his *thank you* sounded forced. He didn't want to thank her. He wanted to have sex with her, right here, on this table.

Jake sighed with relief when she left the room to cook the entree. Picking up his wine, he downed half the glass; he needed to do something to calm the storm raging within him, because if he didn't he might do something he'd bitterly regret in the morning.

'You've really got it bad, haven't you?' Sophie said quietly. 'You implied as much over the phone but seeing it is worth a thousand words.'

Jake glanced over at his sister, who was studying him over the rim of her glass with an intuitive gaze.

'I'll survive,' he returned before swallowing another large gulp of wine.

Sophie smiled knowingly. 'We'll see, Jake. Like I said before, your Abby's gone to a lot of trouble tonight.'

'She's not my Abby. She's still in love with her dead husband.'

'Maybe. But he's dead, Jake. And you're one handsome man.'

Jake sighed. 'Could we stop this conversation right now, please?'

Sophie did stop, but only because Abby entered the dining room carrying with her two plates which exuded the most delicious smell. When she placed his in front of him, Jake saw that it contained a mixture of prawns and scallops over which had been drizzled the source of that tantalising aroma.

'If this tastes as good as it looks,' he said, unable to restrain his admiration for her cooking, 'then we're in for an amazing treat.'

When Jake looked up and saw Abby's delighted face he was consumed with guilt over his earlier bad manners. He hadn't meant to hurt her.

'And, for what it's worth at this late stage,' he added, 'I think that dress you're wearing is stunning. If you ever wear it outside of this house, you'll be fighting the men off with sticks.'

CHAPTER FIFTEEN

ABBY SHOULD HAVE been thrilled with this last compliment. But she wasn't. And the reason was mortifying. Because it was *him* she wanted the chance to fight off, not other men.

Not that she would fight Jake off. Abby knew if he ever made the slightest pass at her, she would be a goner. But he wasn't about to do that, was he? For pity's sake, when was she going to get it through her silly female head that he was just her boss, plus the rather reluctant trustee of his uncle's dying wishes?

If she was brutally honest, it had always been painfully obvious that Jake hadn't wanted to do any of it. Not the car or the money. Or taking her to the grave. But he had, out of a sense of duty, and decency. She meant nothing to him on a personal basis. She was just the person who looked after his house who'd been lucky enough to score a generous legacy from his very kind and thoughtful uncle.

The hurt this realisation brought was very telling, reminding Abby of the various warnings Megan had given her about Jake. But Megan had been wrong. It wasn't Jake she had to worry about but her own silly self. Somewhere along the line she'd started caring about what he thought of her. Started caring for *him*. Which was a total waste of time.

It annoyed Abby that she'd turned into some kind of infatuated fool who fantasised about a man who was way out of her league. As a teenager she'd never had crushes on movie stars or rock stars, and she wasn't about to start now with a television star.

'I'll go get my entree,' she said, and hurried from the room, returning to find that her two guests had waited for her.

The dish was a success, as was the main course, judging by the many compliments she received, plus the evidence of empty plates. Hers weren't quite so empty, her appetite deserting her, as it did when she was emotionally upset over something. She tried not to look at Jake too much or too often, lest he see her feelings for him in her eyes. In the main, she looked at and talked to Sophie, who was quite the conversationalist, one of those women who liked to ask questions, mostly about Abby's likes and dislikes where fashion was concerned. During dessert, however, their conversation turned more personal.

'Jake told me about your husband's death,' Sophie said. 'How tragic for you. He must have been quite young. After all, you're only—what? Mid-twenties?'

'I'm twenty-seven. And, yes, Wayne was only twenty-five when he died. We were the same age.'

'How dreadful for you. And how long had you been married at the time?'

'Four years.'

Sophie's eyebrows arched. 'But no children?'

It was a question which used to cause Abby unbearable pain. It still hurt, but she'd grown to accept that she would never become a mother.

'We were trying,' she said. 'But it just didn't happen.' No way was she going to talk about her three miscarriages. That was way too private. And, yes, way too painful.

'Perhaps it was all for the best,' Sophie said, 'under the circumstances.'

'Perhaps,' Abby choked out.

Jake frowned, having picked up on the raw emotion vibrating in Abby's reply. He recalled he'd said something similar when he'd interviewed her. Suddenly, he saw that it was a tactless remark. He tried to catch Sophie's eye, but she was oblivious to his attempt to put a stop to her queries.

'So, Abby, Jake tells me you want to travel,' his sister continued in her usual blunt fashion.

'Yes. I do.'

'Alone? Or with a friend?'

'Sophie, for pity's sake,' Jake jumped in. 'Stop giving Abby the third degree.'

Sophie gave him a mock innocent look. 'I'm just talking. Okay, change of subject. Jake, how about letting me live in Craig's apartment for a while? Or are you going to sell it?'

'No,' Jake replied slowly. 'I'm not going to sell it. Not yet, anyway. Why do you want to stay there?'

Sophie sighed. 'My flatmate wants to move her boyfriend in and I can't stand him.'

'I see. Well, of course you can stay in Craig's place. I'll give you the keys before you leave.'

'I'll pay you rent,' she offered.

'I don't want any rent. Just pay the electricity bill when it comes in. And don't sublet it to anyone else.'

'I won't. I'm like you, Jake. I like my own space. I should never have shared a flat in the first place. I should have bought one. But I'm just too extravagant to save the deposit. All my money goes on clothes,' she directed at Abby. 'And hair,' she added, patting the chic red bob which flattered her square face.

Jake frowned. 'Craig left you enough for a deposit on a flat, I would have thought.'

'Yes, well, I know he did. But I have other plans for that money. Business plans. So, Abby, you do realise that my brother is going to be shattered when you leave him? He thinks you're the most incredible housekeeper. He never stops raving about you.'

'Really?'

'Really.'

'I'm sure he won't have any trouble finding someone else,' she said.

When her head turned his way, Jake had to use all of his willpower to douse the surge of desire which threatened to unravel him. But he was doomed to failure. He could not stop his eyes from dropping to her mouth, her extremely delicious mouth. How he wanted that mouth; how he wanted *her*!

Abby frowned. Why was Jake staring at her mouth like that? Perhaps she had some food on her lips. When she lifted her napkin from her lap to dab at them, he continued to stare, Abby glimpsing something in his glittering blue eyes which shocked her to the core. It was the way Wayne used to look at her when he wanted sex.

But what shocked Abby the most—aside from the fact that this was Jake lusting after her— was the intensity of her own physical response. Instantly her heart began to race, her belly and nipples tightening in a manner which was both perturbing and insidiously exciting. There was another tightening as well, deep inside her.

When an embarrassing heat threatened to turn her face and neck bright red, Abby quickly stood up.

'I'll go and put the coffee on,' she said, and fled the room.

'Well, well…' Sophie murmured. 'Those weren't the actions of a girl who doesn't fancy you. She's got the hots for you almost as much as you have for her.'

Jake didn't say a word, having been rendered speechless. Because if Sophie was right about Abby then nothing would stop him now. Not his conscience, or anything.

But maybe Sophie was wrong. Maybe Abby had seen the lust in his eyes just now and fled the room in panic.

'I have to get going soon,' Sophie said suddenly. 'I have an early start in the morning.'

Jake gave his sister a narrow-eyed look. 'Doing what?'

'Spending two hours in the gym working off the calories I've consumed tonight. Overweight stylists don't get much work, you know. And don't make a fuss. I'm leaving the path clear for you to finish the evening the way you've been living it in your head for hours. Not that I blame you. She's utterly gorgeous. But possibly a bit fragile after her husband's death. So be careful, Jake. Abby's not your usual type.'

'You think I don't know that?' he snapped. 'Why do you think I've been giving her a wide berth?'

Sophie tipped her head on one side. 'You really care about her, don't you?'

Did he? Jake supposed he did, otherwise he wouldn't have controlled himself this long. But the main reason for that control no longer existed and the dogs of desire he'd been trying to rein in had finally been let loose.

'Do me a favour, will you?' he said abruptly.

'Anything, within reason.'

'Go and tell Abby that you don't want coffee

because you have to go home. Tell her you suffer from migraines and you can feel one coming on.'

Sophie shook her head at him as she stood up. 'I suppose there's a slim chance she might knock you back. But I doubt it,' she added laughingly, then went to do as he'd asked.

CHAPTER SIXTEEN

BY THE TIME Jake walked into the kitchen after
seeing Sophie off, Abby had achieved a measure of control over her wayward body, mostly
by busying herself clearing the table and stack-
ing the dishwasher. Unfortunately, as soon as she
glanced up at him, things started tipping out of
control again.

If only he would stop looking at her like that!

Okay, so Megan had warned her that Jake
might fancy her if she dolled herself up. But she
hadn't really believed her. Until now.

For a long moment Abby just stood there next
to the dishwasher, staring at Jake and thinking that if she let him seduce her—she could
see in his eyes that was what he meant to do—
she would be thrown into a world she was not
equipped to handle. She wasn't like Megan.
She'd never slept with a guy just for the sex.
She'd never wanted to. That was what worried

her the most. How much she wanted to sleep with Jake.

For pity's sake, at least be honest, she castigated herself. You don't want to do any *sleeping* with Jake. You want to have sex with him. But only after you've explored his naked body first, then kissed him all over. You want to do all the things you've read about but never experienced, or even wanted before.

When some shockingly wanton images filled her mind, panic wasn't far behind.

'I… I think I should go home,' she stammered, her cheeks burning with shame.

He shook his head then began walking slowly towards her, closing the dishwasher on the way.

'You can't,' he returned, his voice cool but his eyes still hot. 'You're over the limit.'

He was close now, close enough to reach out and touch her. He softly traced down her nose with one fingertip before slowly encircling her mouth. For a few fraught seconds, Abby held her breath, wide eyes clinging to his, pleading with him not to do this. Or that was what she thought her eyes were doing.

All Jake saw was the dilation of excitement. When her lips finally gasped apart, he smiled. It was a wicked smile, full of satisfaction and arrogance and erotic intent. He meant to have her tonight, and he knew she didn't want to say no.

'Abby, Abby...' he murmured, his voice husky. 'Do you have any idea how much I want you?'

Abby wondered dazedly if he said that to all his women. She had to admit that it was very effective. She shuddered when he pulled her into his arms, squeezing her eyes tightly shut as his head started to descend. The feel of his lips on hers brought a low moan from deep in her throat. When he stopped kissing her, her eyelids fluttered open to find his narrowed eyes scanning hers with concern.

'Tell me you want this too, Abby,' he said. 'Don't go along with me because of gratitude, or because you think you might lose your job if you don't.'

Such thoughts had never entered her head. Nothing much was entering her head at this moment. Nothing but the urgent desire for him to continue. Her lips remained parted as she struggled for breath, her body flushing with a heat which might have been embarrassing if it hadn't been so exciting.

'Tell me you want me to make love to you,' he repeated harshly. '*Say* it.'

Abby swallowed, then licked her lips in an effort to get some moisture into her mouth.

'Yes,' she croaked out.

'Yes, *what*?' he persisted.

'Yes, I... I want you to make love to me.'

He groaned then pulled her even tighter against him, his mouth crashing down on hers with a wild passion which surpassed anything she'd experienced in her marriage. Where Wayne had been gentle and tentative, Jake simply took, invading her mouth with his tongue whilst his hands roved hungrily up and down her spine, one slipping under her hair to capture the back of her neck whilst the other splayed over her bottom. She moaned at the feel of his erection pressing into the soft swell of her stomach, how hard it felt, and her insides contracted in anticipation. She wanted him, not gently, but roughly. Demandingly. She wanted him to fill her. She wanted to come with him inside her.

With a cry of naked need, Abby reefed her mouth from under his, her eyes wide and wild.

'What's wrong?' a stunned Jake asked her.

'Nothing. Everything. Oh, just don't stop, Jake. Please, I... I can't wait.'

Jake didn't need telling twice. He hoisted her up on to the stone counter, ignoring her startled gasp as he reached up under her skirt to remove her panties.

'Lie back,' he commanded as he drew her skirt up and eased her legs apart.

Abby's face flamed with a mad mixture of shame and arousal, sucking in sharply when she felt his hands slide up under her dress to take a firm grasp of her hips, gasping when he slid her forward so that she was right on the edge. She didn't dare look at him, keeping her dilated eyes firmly on the ceiling. But she could feel him, pushing against her hot wet flesh, searching for entry into her oh, so needy body. And then he was there, taking her breath away as yes, he filled her totally. Her head swam when he started up a powerful rhythm, each forward surge of his body bringing her both pleasure and even more frustration. She closed her eyes but nothing could shut out the sounds she started making, moans and pants. Just as she thought she could not bear another moment of such exquisite torment, Abby came, her flesh contracting around his with an electric pleasure that was as stunning as it was violent. Spasm followed spasm, evoking a raw cry from Jake. Then he came too, flooding her for an incredibly long time.

Jake shut his eyes as he wallowed in his glorious release, but it wasn't long before the heat of the moment cooled, and the reality of what he'd just done sunk in, along with the possible consequences.

Jake groaned at his stupidity. After all, the last thing he wanted to be confronted with was an unwanted pregnancy. Which was possible, given he hadn't used a condom.

He really didn't want children, even with a girl like Abby. He enjoyed being free to do as he pleased whenever he pleased. Even one child would put an end to that. Okay, so it was probably selfish of him, but better to be selfish than miserable. He wanted his uncle's lifestyle, not his father's.

When Jake finally opened his eyes, he encountered Abby staring up at him with glazed eyes. Her arms were flopped out wide in the form of a T, her breathing now slow and steady. He did note, however, that her lips remained softly parted as if they were waiting for him to kiss her some more.

He wished he could. But there was no getting away from what he had to do first.

With a sigh he scooped her up and held her close, his face buried into her hair. 'I'm so sorry, Abby,' he murmured with true regret in his voice.

She pulled back a little and blinked up at him. 'For what?'

'I didn't use a condom. But let me assure you,' he raced on when her eyes widened, 'that I'm no risk to you, healthwise. I've always practised safe sex. Till tonight, that is,' he confessed ruefully.

'It's all right, Jake,' she said. 'I can't get pregnant. I'm on the Pill.'

'You are?' He was genuinely surprised. Then relieved. Then curious.

'Don't think I'm not happy about that, but why?' he asked.

She shrugged. 'It gives me control over my body. I don't suffer PMT when I'm on the Pill.'

'So it's not just a birth control thing?'

'No. Though it's as well I am taking it, under the circumstances.'

'I'll say.'

A frown formed on her pretty forehead. 'Can I ask you why you didn't use a condom this time when you say you always practise safe sex?'

Jake didn't want to tell her the truth: that he'd been so crazy with desire for her for so long that stopping to put a condom on would have been impossible, even if he'd thought of it.

He produced a wry little smile as he wrapped her legs around his waist.

'Acute frustration,' he said instead. 'You can blame yourself. You looked so delicious in that dress that I've thought of nothing else but sex all night.'

'Oh...'

Gently, he cupped the back of her head and pulled it down against his chest. His hands stroked up and down her back as they had that day in this very kitchen. But this was hardly the same. Once again, she pulled back and lifted puzzled eyes to his.

'Is...is it always like that for your women?' she asked him.

Jake was somewhat taken aback. What exactly did she mean? Did his lovers always come? Did they come the way she'd just come? Like a woman who hadn't had a climax in years.

'Not always,' he said. 'Not all people click, sexually.'

She nodded at his answer. 'But we do. Click sexually, I mean.'

He smiled again. 'Very much so. We're going to have a great time together.'

'But...what about your girlfriend?' She needed to be sure he wasn't cheating with her.

'I broke up with Olivia some time ago.'

'I see,' she said thoughtfully. 'Yes, I see.'

Jake wasn't sure what she saw. He wasn't all that keen on the way women liked to analyse everything. He didn't want to have a post-mortem of why the sex between them was so good. He wanted to get back to some serious lovemaking. In bed next time. He just wanted Abby naked in his bed where he could make slow love to her for hours.

He didn't withdraw. He just scooped her up from the breakfast bar, holding her tightly as he headed for the stairs, their fused and very wet flesh reminding Jake once more that he hadn't used a condom. Walking up stairs while still inside her was doing things to him which should have been impossible, given he'd just had the most satisfying climax.

And wow it felt good. *She* felt good. Maybe he'd just forget the condoms for tonight. After all, they'd already done it once. Might as well be hanged for a sheep as a lamb, as they said. From tomorrow he'd go back to being super careful. Tonight, however, he would indulge himself to the full.

CHAPTER SEVENTEEN

ABBY HAD BEEN right about not wanting to actually *sleep* with Jake. She didn't. She couldn't. Every nerve-ending in her body was still electrified. *He'd* finally fallen asleep, however. It wasn't surprising after two hours of almost constant sexual activity. Abby had lost count of how many times she'd come, Jake showing her that a woman's capacity for orgasms far surpassed a man's, especially when said woman was being made love to by a man of his experience. He knew exactly where to touch. What to touch. How to touch.

Abby closed her eyes as she relived all that he'd done to her. First there had been that incredible episode on the kitchen counter. That had been amazing enough. But not as sensational as once they were both naked in bed together. After another incredible orgasm, just when she'd thought she couldn't bear any more, he'd carried her into the shower and revived her under some cool jets of water. After drying her off, he'd carried her back to bed, where some more kissing and caressing had soon had her trembling with desire again. His own flesh had been solidly re-aroused also, the size of him astonishing her at times. But always bringing her the most exquisite pleasure.

Such thinking sent Abby's eyes over to Jake, who was lying face down on the bed, sound asleep. She stared at his back, which had several red tracks where her nails had raked over his skin. She shook her head at the savagery of her passion for Jake. Not to mention her stupidity. What had possessed her to admit she was on the Pill? Her brain knew it was a risk to have sex without a condom, despite his reassurances. But her body hadn't cared. In truth, she would have let him continue even if she *hadn't* been on the Pill. Which was insane! Just the thought of falling pregnant made her feel ill. She could not go there again. Not now. Not ever. It had hurt too much each time a baby had been wrenched from her body. More so because she'd wanted a child so much. Or she had, back then when she'd been married to Wayne. No way did she want Jake Sanderson's child. He didn't want a child, either. Or did he think he would simply pay her to have an abortion if the Pill failed and she got pregnant? Which it might. The Pill wasn't one hundred per cent safe.

A ghastly thought suddenly crossed her mind, propelling her from the bed. With a groan she hurried into the bathroom, where she wrapped a bath sheet around herself, intent on getting downstairs as quickly as possible to make sure she'd taken her Pill for the evening. Now that she thought about it, she couldn't actually remember taking it. *Oh, God!*

Abby didn't make it past the foot of the bed before Jake stirred.

'Abby?' came his slurred voice.

She froze as his right arm stretched out, feeling for her. Finding the bed empty, he rolled over and sat up.

'Where do you think you're going?' he asked.

'Downstairs,' she answered in an astonishingly calm voice. 'I… I have to check on something.'

He frowned. 'What?'

'I suddenly had this awful feeling I might have forgotten to take my Pill earlier. But if I have, please don't worry. I'll get the morning-after pill. I don't want to have a baby any more than you do. But from now we should use condoms. The Pill I take is a good one but no Pill is one hundred per cent safe.'

He nodded. 'Very true. Okay, from now on, we'll use condoms. After all, we don't want any unfortunate accidents, do we?'

Abby swallowed. 'No,' she said, thinking that surely fate wouldn't be that cruel to her. She always took her Pill around six-thirty. She glanced at the digital clock sitting on her side of the bed. Ten to one.

But she was getting ahead of herself, Abby realised. What she needed to do was get herself downstairs and check.

'I won't be long,' she said, and bolted for the door and the stairs, heading for the kitchen where she'd left her new bag on the counter-top next to the microwave. Ten seconds later she was almost sobbing with relief, as she saw the punched through dome where the day's Pill had sat. Thank heavens, she thought, though her heart was still racing. What she needed, she realised, was something to calm her down. Not coffee. Some wine perhaps.

A minute later, Abby hurried back up the stairs, carrying with her the bottle of dessert wine they'd hardly touched at dinner, along with two glasses. Hopefully, she didn't look as horrified at herself as she suddenly felt. In a matter of hours Jake had turned her into...what? A woman with needs—needs which this man could obviously satisfy.

The bed was empty when she entered the bedroom, Jake simultaneously walking back into the room from the bathroom. But where she had a towel wrapped modestly around her, he was stark naked.

Abby liked that she now felt free to ogle him. For he was a man worth ogling: magnificently built with broad shoulders, flat stomach, slim hips and long strong legs. His skin was naturally olive, his body hair dark but not overly abundant. It was thickest in the middle of his chest, arrowing down to his groin. Abby gazed at that part of him which she admired and desired the most. She hadn't kissed him there yet. But she wanted to.

'It's all right,' she said straight away. 'Pill all safely taken.'

'Fantastic. Now, why don't you dispense with that towel, wench?' he said as he climbed back on to the bed, sitting up with pillows stuffed behind his back.

'Can't,' Abby replied rather breathlessly. How easy it was for him to turn her on. 'My hands are full.'

'Then come closer and I'll do it for you,' he said, his smile quite wicked.

Her head spun as she approached his side of the bed, waiting there like a good little wench till he reached out and peeled the towel from her body. His gaze was hot and hungry as it travelled over her, lingering on her breasts till she could actually feel her erect nipples tingling with anticipation.

'Give the bottle to me,' he commanded.

She did so. He placed it on the bedside table.

'Now the glasses,' he added.

She handed them over and he filled each one halfway, handing one back to her.

'Drink,' he ordered, and she did, downing all of it.

He didn't drink any of his, putting the glass down next to the bottle. Abby stared when he dipped his finger in the chilled wine then reached out to dab it over her nearest nipple.

She gasped.

'You like that?' he asked throatily and she nodded, her tongue feeling thick in her throat.

'Come,' he said, taking the empty glass out of her hand and putting it down before drawing her back on to the bed. Not on her side, but on his, sitting her down first then tipping her back across his thighs.

When Abby stared up at him with stunned eyes, Jake knew then that she was as innocent as he'd always feared. Up until this point he hadn't been absolutely sure. The way she'd insisted on a quickie down on the kitchen counter hadn't smacked of innocence.

But it was obvious that no one had ever dabbed wine on her nipples before, let alone her clitoris. Her surprise delighted and excited him. He dabbed some wine on her other nipple before pulling her on to the bed so that he could bend his mouth to her very beautiful breasts. He loved the way she moaned when he sucked her nipples deep into his mouth. Loved the way she couldn't seem to stop him from doing whatever he wanted. He liked her lack of experience, but at the same time it worried him. If he wasn't careful she might fall in love with him, which was the last thing he wanted.

CHAPTER EIGHTEEN

ABBY LOVED THE feel of his mouth on her breast. Loved it when he lapped gently at her nipple. Loved it even more when he nipped it with his teeth. She groaned when his head lifted abruptly, not wanting him to stop.

'What's wrong?' she said when she saw his frown.

His intense gaze grew quite frustrated. 'I don't know why I'm going to say this but I am. You won't be silly and fall in love with me, will you, Abby?'

Abby could not have been more taken aback, her focus tonight having been all on her sexual feelings, not romantic ones. Still, once she thought about it, she could see that it would be easy for her to become seriously infatuated with Jake. But love? It was difficult to fall in love with a man who'd shown no interest in her till circumstance had thrown them into each other's company, coincidentally at the same time he'd broken up with his current girlfriend.

Abby wasn't a fool. She could see that his suddenly fancying her was very convenient to Jake, that was all. He wanted her, but only because she was there. And pretty enough to interest him. Wayne, however, had wanted her from the first moment he'd clapped eyes on her, stained teeth and all. Her husband might not have set her heart racing the way Jake could, but he'd been a man worth loving. Abby could never truly love a man who was only sexually attracted to her. That kind of man would never capture her heart and soul.

'I'm not interested in marriage and children,' he told her, cementing any possible doubts she might have about loving him.

'I know that, Jake,' she replied a little coolly. 'You don't have to spell it out for me. Your reputation precedes you. I'm not interested in marriage and children, either. I don't want anything from you but sex, so you don't have to worry.'

He blinked his surprise at her.

'It's true,' she said, nodding as she thought about what her sister would say to her.

You've discovered the pleasures of the flesh at last, hon. Enjoy it whilst it's on offer. Because a man like Jake will move on after a while.

Thinking of her sister's probable advice confirmed in Abby's mind what she was feeling for Jake. This was sex, not love.

'I assure you I won't fall in love with you.' In lust maybe, but never in love.

His laugh was dry. 'I guess I asked for that. But you don't have to sound so sure. That's not very flattering.'

'Sorry.'

He smiled wryly. 'No need to apologise. I appreciate honesty. Now, where was I?'

Before he could bend his mouth once more to her breast, Abby sat up. She no longer wanted him to do that. She wanted to do things to *him*.

'Jake,' she said sharply, her eyes a bit nervous as they met his.

He frowned again. 'What now?'

'Since you like honesty, can I be honest with you about something else?'

'Be my guest,' he said, leaning back against the pillows.

Abby swallowed then gathered her courage to get out what she wanted to say. 'The thing is, I've…um…only been with one man before you. My husband. I loved Wayne dearly but I…we… well, I don't think I clicked sexually with him the way I do with you. I've never come before, during sex. I mean I've come but not during actual intercourse. I've also never done some other things that I've read about and which I feel I... um...would like to do with you.'

It hadn't been easy admitting all that, especially with Jake's eyes on her all the while, mainly because she couldn't read his expression. Surely he couldn't be *pleased* with her confession. She would have thought he liked his women very experienced.

'I see,' he said rather cryptically. 'What kind of things?'

She tried not to blush. She couldn't imagine Jake liking women who blushed. Gritting her teeth, Abby resolved to continue telling him the truth without surrendering to silly schoolgirl nerves.

'Well, oral sex, for starters. That's one thing I'd like to do. But I want to do it properly. I was hoping you might show me how.'

CHAPTER NINETEEN

ABBY WOKE SLOWLY, awareness of her physical well-being seeping into her brain before she remembered whose bed she was in, plus everything she had done in it the night before.

'Oh,' she cried, sitting up abruptly in what proved to be a blessedly empty bed. Lord knew how she would have coped if Jake had been lying there beside her, bearing witness to her very fierce embarrassment.

What had seemed so natural—so *right*—last night, now seemed very wrong. And very decadent. It blew Abby's mind that she had told Jake she'd never come during sex before. As for her telling him she wanted him to teach her how to go down on him…

She might have sat there, castigating herself for ages if the man himself hadn't walked back into the room, holding two mugs of steaming coffee and smiling at her with genuine warmth in his eyes. He wasn't naked, thank heavens, though he was only wearing jeans, his chest still bare.

As was hers, she realised, snatching up the sheet to cover her breasts.

'Now, now,' Jake chided with dancing blue eyes as he approached her side of the bed. 'None of that false modesty this morning, thank you. I've already seen your beautiful breasts at close quarters. Not to mention the rest of your very lovely body.'

His compliments went some way to soothing her embarrassment, as did his totally natural manner. Abby realised that if she wanted to continue having sex with Jake—and she very definitely did—then she had to get her head around the way he expected his women to act. At the same time, she wasn't about to turn into some kind of exhibitionist.

'Well, that was last night,' she returned, keeping the sheet where it was. 'I don't like swanning around with no clothes on in the daytime.'

'How do you know?' he said, placing one of the mugs on the bedside table next to her. 'Maybe you should try it some time.'

Abby wondered if it had been a mistake telling him so much about her past sex life. It worried her that Jake might think he had a licence to do anything and everything with her.

He frowned at her as he sat down on her side of the bed. 'I have a feeling that you're suffering from a severe case of the morning afters.'

Abby shrugged, then carefully picked up the very hot mug with one hand whilst keeping the sheet in place with her other hand.

'Probably,' she admitted after taking a small sip.

'What's worrying you?'

She took another sip of coffee, mulling over what to say.

'I guess I just don't know how to act this morning,' she said at last. 'I mean…it's an awkward situation, with me being your housekeeper.'

'I think it's anything but awkward,' he said, smiling a wickedly sexy smile. 'It's very convenient that you're already here, in my house, every day.'

'I'm not going to be your secret mistress, Jake,' she warned him, despite suspecting that she would be whatever he wanted her to be. Provided he kept having sex with her.

'You can't be my secret mistress,' he said, the corners of his mouth twitching. 'I'm not married.'

She glowered up at him. 'Secret lover, then!'

'Okay,' he said. 'Fair enough. How about you just become my girlfriend? Nothing secretive. All above board. If you like, I'll tell the world on next Monday's show. Or, better still, I'll put it on Twitter this very day. *My gorgeous young housekeeper and I are now an item.'*

Abby looked horrified. 'Don't you dare!'

Jake's eyebrows lifted. 'Is there any reason why I shouldn't?'

'My sister is addicted to Twitter. *And* your show.'

Now his brows beetled together. 'You don't want your sister to know we're an item?'

'No!'

'Why not? Will she be shocked?'

Hardly, Abby thought, since Megan had warned her that this might happen.

Abby sighed. 'Probably not,' she admitted. 'But she'll go on and on about it. She'll want to know the ins and outs of everything, and I'm just not ready to answer all her questions at this stage.'

'So I'm to be *your* secret lover, am I?'

Only then did Abby realise that that was exactly what she wanted him to be. She simply wasn't ready to share this incredible experience with anyone else. She didn't want to risk spoiling anything. She didn't want a cynical Megan telling her not to expect their relationship to last. Not that it was a *relationship*. It was just sex.

'Would you mind?' she asked him, shocked by her own boldness.

Jake actually did mind. Quite a bit. He didn't like the thought that Abby wanted to treat him as a sexual object rather than a proper boyfriend. Which was ironic, considering that was what he'd done in reverse for years—treated women more as sexual objects rather than proper girl-friends.

But he could see no pluses in arguing with her just now.

'If that's what you want,' he said with a non-chalant shrug of his shoulders.

She stared at him. 'You're very easy-going, aren't you?'

'Very,' he lied, deciding this was the way to play the game for a while. Give her what she wanted. Though he had no intention of being her secret lover for long. That was not what *he* wanted. 'Now, how about I take you away some-where for the weekend? In the Ferrari. You can do some of the driving,' he offered with a dev-ilish grin.

'I'd love to,' she said excitedly. 'But won't you

be recognised if we go anywhere in public together?'

'Maybe. Maybe not. Sunglasses and a baseball cap go a long way to disguising one's identity. But I'll certainly be recognised once I book us into a place for the night. The name on my credit card will give the game away. But *your* identity can be kept a secret. For a while. But only for a while, I suspect. The truth will out in the end, Abby. Your sister will find out eventually, even if you don't tell her. The media has long and very tenacious tentacles. So I would suggest that when we get back on Sunday evening, you give her a call.'

'We'll see,' she said, still not happy at the thought of telling Megan about them.

Abby couldn't deny she was flattered that Jake actually *wanted* her to be his girlfriend. But, if truth be told, she didn't feel adequate for such a role. She wasn't well educated, or well travelled. Hardly a woman of the world in the bedroom, either. Still, maybe that was what he liked about her, the way Max de Winter liked the heroine in *Rebecca*—because she was the total opposite of his dead but highly decadent wife. Maybe it was Abby's own ordinariness that appealed to Jake after having a string of over-achieving, super-glamorous girlfriends.

Of course, he wasn't about to propose, as the hero did in *Rebecca*. Aside from the fact that Jake was anti-marriage, men these days didn't have to marry to enjoy the pleasures of the flesh. Neither did women, Abby conceded, a highly erotic shiver running down her spine as she looked at Jake's beautiful male body. She could hardly wait to have it all to herself again. There was so much more she had to learn. So many more things she had yet to try.

'Keep looking at me like that, sweetheart,' Jake said drily, 'and we won't even get out of this house today.'

CHAPTER TWENTY

WHEN ABBY BLUSHED, Jake stood up abruptly before he gave in to temptation and made his last words come true. As exciting as sex with Abby was, he didn't want to confine their relationship to a strictly sexual one. He wanted her company out of the bedroom as well. He wanted to show her all the places she'd never been before. Wanted to share with her all the wonders the world had to offer.

This last thought jolted him a bit. He'd never travelled overseas with a female companion before. Nothing beyond a few days in some fancy South Seas resort, that was. But he wanted to with Abby. And he was done with that silly show of his. It actually annoyed him that he couldn't go anywhere these days without being recognised. He pretended he didn't mind to Abby but the truth was it irritated him to death.

So the decision was made. He would sell the

show ASAP and do something more exciting and fulfilling with his life. But first things first.

'I'll go fix us both some breakfast while you get showered and dressed,' he said. 'Then we're heading north. Port Macquarie, maybe. That's a decent drive. Have you ever been there before?'

She shook her head. 'I've never been out of Sydney. No, that's not true. I went on a school excursion to Canberra once when I was twelve.'

'And what did you think of our capital?'

'Can't remember it much. I was only there for two days and I froze to death the whole time.'

'It's much nicer at this time of year. Would you like to go there instead?'

'I don't really mind where we go,' she said. 'You decide.'

'Canberra it is, then.'

'You'll have to take me home first,' Abby told him hurriedly. 'I'll need to change and get some more clothes. I only have the dress with me that I wore last night. And I'll have to get some overnight things.'

'Fair enough. We won't get waylaid by your next-door neighbour, will we?'

'Harriet doesn't get up till lunchtime on a Saturday.'

'We should be long gone by then. Now, hop to it, Abby. Patience is not one of my virtues.'

'What are your virtues?' she asked, her eyes sparkling with uncharacteristic mischief.

Jake shrugged. 'Not sure. Honesty, I suppose. And integrity. Now, no more chit-chat. Up!' he ordered as he strode purposefully from the room.

Abby sat there a few seconds longer, thinking that there was more to Jake's virtues than honesty and integrity. He was also generous and caring. She liked that he'd loved his uncle as much as he had. Liked the way he'd fulfilled his uncle's dying wishes, even though he'd obviously found her a nuisance at first.

Not so much a nuisance now, she thought, a rather naughty smile pulling at her lips.

'I can't hear the shower running!' Jake called up the stairs, his voice echoing in the quiet house.

'Just going now,' Abby called back, putting the mug down and throwing back the doona.

Abby never sang in the shower. But she did that day, feeling even happier than when she'd got her porcelain veneers. Nothing could compare with the delicious lightness of spirit which was surging through her veins at that moment. She could not recall ever feeling so exhilarated. Or so excited. It did cross her mind for a split second that she might be falling in love with Jake, but she immediately dismissed the idea as fanciful. She liked him very much. And lusted after him a lot. But that was the sum total of her feelings at this stage.

She did concede later, as she ate the fantastic breakfast Jake had cooked, that her feelings for him might deepen if he kept on spoiling her this way.

But she would not worry about that today. Today was to be devoted to having the kind of carefree fun she'd never had before. She might even get to drive a Ferrari. How incredible was that?

'You're quite a good cook,' Abby complimented him.

'I can do the basics like steak and salad, and bacon and eggs. But I could never cook anything like you did last night. That meal was marvellous, Abby.'

'It wasn't all that special,' she said, trying to be modest.

'I thought it was. And so did Sophie.'

'I liked your sister, Jake. You're very close, aren't you?'

'Yes. Much closer than my other siblings. Sophie are I are the loners in the family. The rest are all married with children.'

'Goodness. That must make for a big group at Christmas. Do they all live here in Sydney?'

'Yep. And you're right about Christmas. I've already hired a boat for a cruise on the harbour this year. No one's house can accommodate everyone, except when some of them go to the in-laws. Which apparently isn't happening this year. What about you, Abby? How many in your family?'

'Just me and Megan. And little Timmy, of course.'

'What about your parents?' Jake asked, curious about Abby's family now.

'They're dead. Dad got killed in a fight when I was seventeen. Mum died of an accidental overdose a few months later.'

Jake was taken aback by Abby's matter-of-fact relaying of what must have affected her badly at the time. 'That's very sad, Abby.'

'I suppose so. But truly, they were terrible parents. Always down at the pub. There was never enough money for me and Megan. All they loved was alcohol.'

Jake tried not to look too shocked at Abby's truly ghastly background. Poor thing. She'd had it really tough. No wonder she'd got married young. Probably wanted some man to look after her and love her. Which obviously this Wayne had before he'd died too.

Abby didn't like Jake's silence. No doubt he thought she came from a low-life family. He was probably regretting asking a girl like her to be his girlfriend. 'It's not a pretty story, is it?' she said, a bit defiantly.

'I admire the way you survived it with the lovely nature that you have,' he said gently.

Abby blinked rapidly as moisture suddenly pooled in her eyes.

'You're not going to cry, are you?' Jake asked, alarm in his voice.

Abby almost laughed. Clearly, he didn't like his girlfriends to cry. Which was perverse since she was sure every one of them cried buckets when he broke up with them. Which he always did. Eventually.

It was a sobering thought, and one which she vowed never to forget.

'No,' she said with creditable calm. 'I'm not going to cry. Now, why don't I clear up here whilst you go and get ready? Oh, and Jake...'

'Yes?'

'Um…don't forget to pack some condoms.'

Was he startled by her very practical request? Or annoyed?

Abby imagined that he didn't want to use condoms. Neither did she, if she were honest. But she refused to lose her head totally over Jake.

'How many should I pack?' he asked, his tone as provocative as his glittering blue eyes.

'How many do you have in the house?' she countered, constantly surprised at her boldness. Surprised but not displeased. Abby suspected she was going to like her new bolder self.

'Not sure,' Jake replied thoughtfully. 'There's one unopened box in the bathroom upstairs, as well as a few loose ones in the top drawers of both bedside tables. There's a couple more in the glovebox of my car and two more in my wallet. So a rough estimate would be about two dozen. How many do you think we might need?'

Abby kept a straight face with difficulty. The man was a wicked devil all right.

'Don't ask me,' she said, brilliantly po-faced. 'I only have last night to go by and that might have been a one-off for you. I would imagine a man can get it up quite a bit with a woman during their first night together. But after that, things might very well go downhill. It's not as though you're a teenager, Jake, or even in your twenties. Which reminds me, how old *are* you? Late thirties? Early forties?'

Jake glowered at her for a long moment before shaking his head then smiling a drily amused smile.

'You're teasing me, aren't you?'

'No more than you teased me.'

'Fair enough. And, since you asked, I'm thirty-four. Which makes me still in my prime. So watch yourself tonight. You might find yourself begging me to stop before I'm finished.'

Abby feigned a disappointed face. 'You mean I have to wait till tonight?'

Jake wagged a finger at her. 'I should call your bluff. But I won't. Now, let's get going.'

CHAPTER TWENTY-ONE

'YOU'RE RIGHT,' ABBY said, closing her eyes as she leant back, her hair flying free. 'Riding in this car with the top down is amazing. I would do this every day if I could.'

'Sorry. Weekend treat only. Next time we *will* head north to Port Macquarie.'

Abby opened her eyes as her head turned towards Jake. 'I wouldn't mind where I go,' she said. 'As long as it's in this gorgeous car.'

And as long as I'm with you.

'Great. Now, do you want to stop somewhere for lunch or just go straight to Canberra?'

'No,' Abby said straight away. 'I don't want to stop. Not unless you do. I'm not hungry at all. We can have something to eat when we get to Canberra.'

'A girl after my own heart,' he said with a warm smile thrown her way.

Abby's own heart twisted with his remark, because there was no point in her being after his heart. All Jake wanted from a woman was her body in bed, and her company when out of bed. He obviously liked having a steady girlfriend. Much more convenient for his lifestyle. What he didn't want was for his girlfriends to want more from him than he was prepared to give. Clearly, whenever a girlfriend started looking for more they were out of the door.

Abby realised she would only have herself to blame if she started wanting more. Forewarned was forearmed.

To give Jake credit, he'd been honest with her about his intentions. Or lack of them. She recalled he'd listed honesty as one of his virtues. Integrity as well. Which meant he wouldn't have lied to her about not being a risk to her health when he didn't use a condom.

Thinking of condoms brought Abby's mind back to the incredible climaxes she'd had with Jake last night. She hadn't known till then that such pleasure existed. Whenever Megan raved on about how much she enjoyed sex—how much she actually *needed* it at times—Abby had thought her some kind of nymphomaniac. Now, she appreciated where her sister was coming from. Abby felt sure that by tonight she would very definitely be needing sex with Jake. Already she could feel herself responding to just the thought of being with him, desire invading her body from her curling toes right up to her spinning head. Waiting till tonight was almost beyond bearing. But she *would* wait. No way was she going to humiliate herself by throwing herself at him any earlier.

Abby turned her head just enough so that she could at least have the pleasure of looking at him.

He was wearing stonewashed grey jeans and a white polo top, along with sunglasses and a black baseball cap which did, thankfully, make him more difficult to identify as Jake Sanderson, famed television host and one of Sydney's most recognisable personalities.

Abby didn't want to share him with his adoring public today. Or any other day, for that matter. She couldn't think of anything worse than having strangers come up to them all the time, asking Jake for his autograph. She certainly didn't like the thought of people looking at *her* and wondering what on earth Jake was doing with such a nobody.

Not that she wasn't attractive, especially now that she was dressing better and wearing make-up. Jake, however, was the type of man who dated movie stars and supermodels, or at the very least glamorous newsreaders who were instantly recognisable. They were also women who didn't wear clothes from bargain basement stores. When she'd put on the same outfit this morning that she'd worn when Jake had taken her car shopping last week, Abby had been happy enough with the way she looked. She'd thought—possibly mistakenly—that her tight white pants and spotty top looked quite classy and not cheap. But maybe she'd been deluding herself.

Abby jerked her head round to stare out of the passenger window, not liking that she was suddenly losing confidence in herself. I *do* look good, she told herself firmly. Stop with the worrying.

But the worries continued. Not with her appearance but with what Megan would say when she rang her sister on Sunday night and confessed all. As much as she would like to keep Jake as her secret lover, she could see he wasn't going to allow that to happen.

No doubt Megan would say 'I told you so' in the most irritatingly smug way. She wouldn't be shocked. Well, not about the sex part. She would, however, be shocked that Jake wanted her to be his girlfriend. Abby could just imagine Megan's reaction to that. It would be pure cynicism.

Abby wasn't looking forward to that conversation one little bit. She wanted to enjoy her time with Jake. The last thing she needed was her cynical sister telling her it was only a temporary role. For heaven's sake, she already knew that. She might not be a genius, but she wasn't stupid. Okay, so it was inevitable that one day she would get her marching orders. Abby resolved that she would face that moment when it came. Meanwhile, she aimed to live for the moment. Wasn't that what those lifestyle gurus were always advocating? Not to worry about the past or the future but to seize the moment. Well, at the moment she was in this gorgeous car with a gorgeous man and she wasn't going to let anybody or anything spoil things for her.

Famous last words, Abby thought, and heaved a huge sigh.

'Would you like me to put on some music?' Jake offered, perhaps thinking that her sigh meant she was bored.

'No, thanks,' she replied with a quick smile his way. 'I just want to relax and enjoy the scenery.' Plus try very hard to just live in the moment.

'Actually, the scenery's not that good. That's

the trouble with motorways. They bypass the interesting bits.'

'I don't really care about the scenery. I'm just enjoying the ride. And the company,' she added smilingly.

CHAPTER TWENTY-TWO

ME TOO, JAKE THOUGHT, confirming his earlier idea about taking Abby overseas with him. Not that he would mention it to her just yet. It was too soon. Not for him. For her.

'Would you mind if I asked you something?' he said.

'That depends, I guess, on what it is.'

'Nothing too personal. While I was waiting for you at your place this morning, I saw a big pile of books on your coffee table in the living room. I couldn't help noticing that they included some of my uncle's favourite novels, which reminded me that you asked me if he'd left you books in his will. Am I right in presuming he gave you those books?'

'Actually, no, he didn't. But he did give me a list of books which he said any self-respecting female should read. I bought them myself from a secondhand book shop.'

'I see. And have you read them all yet?'

'I'm on the last one now. *Rebecca*.'

'And which ones are your favourites?'

'Goodness, that's a hard question. I liked them all. But I guess not equally. I'd already read three of them at school. *Pride and Prejudice* and *Wuthering Heights* and *Jane Eyre*. Oh, and I've seen about three movie versions of *Great Expectations*, so I knew what was going to happen, which half spoils a story, doesn't it? Though I can see now how brilliantly written they all were. Difficult to pick out just one. Hmm… I adored *Shōgun*. What a fantastic story with a fantastic hero! *The Fountainhead* was riveting stuff too, though the main characters were a bit OTT, in my opinion.'

'I couldn't agree more,' Jake said. 'What did you think of *To Kill a Mockingbird*?'

'Oh, that was a wonderful story. It made me cry buckets. So did *Anna Karenina*. That poor sad lady.'

'So you don't have an all-time favourite?'

'Not really. Though it might be *Rebecca*, as long as it finishes well.'

'What part are you up to?'

'She's about to come down the stairs dressed in that same outfit Rebecca wore, and I just *know* Max is not going to be very happy.'

Jake had to smile. 'You can say that again. Actually, you've quite a bit more to go. And a few more surprises to come.'

'Don't you dare tell me anything!'

'Obviously you haven't seen the movie version.'

'No. I didn't know there was one.'

'Yes, it was made in nineteen forty, only two years after the book was published. Alfred Hitchcock directed it. Laurence Olivier played Max and Joan Fontaine was the unnamed heroine. I'll get a copy for you after you've finished the book.'

Her face carried a touching mixture of disbelief and excitement. 'Would you really?'

'Of course.'

'But where would you get a copy from?'

'You can get just about everything over the internet these days.'

Happiness radiated from her truly lovely green eyes. 'Would you watch it with me?'

'It would be my pleasure. It's a great film. Craig loved it, though not as much as the book.'

'Your uncle was an incredibly well-read man, wasn't he?'

'Yes. And he read books right across the spectrum from literary works to popular fiction. He was the same with music. He absolutely adored the classical composers, but he loved all music, from Country and Western to rock and even rap. There wasn't a snobbish bone in his body.'

'You loved him a lot, didn't you?'

Jake's heart squeezed tight in his chest. He scooped in a deep breath then let it out slowly. 'I'm still angry with him for not telling me he was terminally ill.'

Abby nodded. 'You're right. He should have told you.'

Jake shrugged, not wanting to spoil their weekend together by talking about sad things. Thinking of Craig, however, had reminded Jake of what his uncle had told him in that last letter, about living life to the full. Suddenly, he didn't want to wait to take Abby overseas with him. Time to seize the day!

'Do you have a passport, Abby?' he asked.

'What?'

'A passport. Do you have a passport?'

'No. Why?'

'You're going to need one when we go to Hawaii in January.'

She blinked over at him. 'Are you serious? You want me to go to Hawaii with you?'

'Not just Hawaii. I also want to take you to

mainland America. California first, and possibly Vegas, then later over to New York. After New York, we'll go on to Europe, but only after the weather turns kinder. Europe in the winter is not for a girl who's never been out of Australia.'

'But…but…don't you have to be here in Sydney to do your show?'

'No. I don't want to do it any more. I'm going to sell it. I have a buyer who's been after the show for ages. You're going to love Europe, Abby,' he swept on, feeling the excitement already building. 'And Asia. Especially Japan.'

When he glanced over at her, she was shaking her head at him, her expression troubled. 'Maybe by January you won't want to take me anywhere.'

Jake could not have been more startled. 'And why would that be?'

'You might grow bored with me.'

He smiled over at her. 'I find that highly unlikely. What's the matter, Abby? Don't you want to go?'

'Yes,' she said after a heart-stopping space of time. 'Of course I do. It's just that…'

'Just that what?'

'What if you grow bored with me when we're overseas? You won't dump me in some strange city, will you?'

Jake was so shocked he almost ran off the road. As it was, he hit the shoulder, sending gravel spurting out behind them.

'Hell, Abby, what kind of man do you think I am?' he threw at her once he'd righted the car. 'I would never do anything like that. And I won't grow bored with you. Where on earth is all this talk of boredom coming from?'

'According to Megan your girlfriends don't last very long.'

Jake rolled his eyes, inwardly cursing the tabloids for reporting every time one of his relationships broke up, even the ones that never really got off the ground. They made him sound like a playboy of the worst kind. He realised Abby would take some convincing that he wasn't that bad.

'Firstly, let me say that it's not always me who ends the relationships. The women I've dated always claim they don't want marriage, but in the end they do. That's a deal breaker for me, Abby. You sounded very sure last night when you said you didn't want to get married again and I believed you. Was I right to believe you?'

'Absolutely,' she said with a little shudder.

Jake still couldn't make up his mind whether her aversion to marrying again was because she'd loved her husband too much to contemplate marriage to another man, or because her dead husband had done something to turn her off the institution.

He decided to find out.

'But why *is* that, Abby?' he asked. 'What happened to turn you off the idea of remarrying?'

CHAPTER TWENTY-THREE

ABBY STIFFENED. SHE hadn't expected their conversation to take this path. She hadn't expected Jake to offer to take her overseas, either. She certainly hadn't expected him to ask her to explain why she didn't want to get married again.

Clearly, she would have to tell him something, or he might rescind his offer. The thought of travelling to all those exciting places with Jake was way too tempting. But what to say? Not the truth, that was for sure. Just when she was getting desperate, Abby remembered something she'd recently read.

'If you must know, my reason is like what Scarlet told Rhett in *Gone with the Wind*, when he asked her to marry him.'

Jake frowned. 'Sorry. I can't remember what she said. Enlighten me.'

'She said she didn't *like* being married.'

'Ah, yes, I remember now. But Abby, that reason was about her not enjoying sex. Maybe you didn't enjoy sex with your husband but you sure as hell enjoy it with me.'

Which means, Jake thought, that she might change her mind at some future date and want to marry him.

'No, no, you've got the wrong end of the stick,' Abby said firmly before he could explore that rather worrying thought. 'It's not the sex part of marriage that disappointed me. Not really. I quite liked sex with Wayne, even if I didn't come the way I do with you. What I didn't like was my loss of independence, plus my total loss of freedom. In the beginning, I thought I wanted to be an old-fashioned housewife, but the truth is I was just running away from life because I had no self-esteem. I thought I would be happy staying at home twenty-four-seven and being a good little wife and mother. Wayne was a very nice man and he loved me to death, bad teeth and all. But in the end I wasn't happy.'

Which was a huge understatement, Abby thought as she swallowed the lump in her throat then gritted her teeth so she wouldn't cry.

'I'm glad now that we didn't have children,' she lied. 'Once I got over my grief I decided I had to get out there and get myself a job. But first I had to get my teeth fixed or I simply wouldn't have the confidence to go for an interview. Not that I was all that confident when I first showed up at your house,' she added with a rueful little laugh.

'You were a bit nervous,' Jake admitted.

'I was surprised when you gave me the job. Surprised and grateful. It did wonders for my self-esteem. But it was meeting your uncle, Jake, which changed me the most, not just on the outside but on the inside. He made me see myself as an intelligent woman with a lot of potential. He made me braver. It was wonderful of him to give me a new car and some travel money, but his legacy is much more than that. The old Abby would never have dared go to bed with you last night or come away with you this weekend, let alone contemplate going overseas with you. The new more adventurous Abby, however, simply can't say no. I want to do all the things I've never done before—to go places I've never been before. I want to be carefree, not committed. I want to have fun. Is that terribly selfish of me?'

'Hardly, since it's the credo I live by. Why do you think I don't want marriage and children? During my growing up years I witnessed two ways of life with my father and my uncle. When my father died at forty-seven, a worn-out shell of a man, I knew which one I would choose. I was only a teenager when I made a conscious decision to live the life of a bachelor and I've been very happy doing that.'

Up till now, came a sudden and rather perturbing thought. He eased off the accelerator as he brought his attention back to the road.

'If ever there was a car designed to corrupt it's this little baby,' he said ruefully.

'Same as its owner then,' Abby quipped.

Jake's eyebrows shot upwards. 'You think I've corrupted you?'

Abby smiled. 'Don't sound so shocked, Jake. Of course you've corrupted me. And I dare say you haven't finished yet. But not to worry, I'm enjoying every single moment.'

Their eyes locked, Abby finding it difficult to maintain her saucy attitude in the face of Jake's intense gaze. She could talk big all she liked but underneath her bold facade the old Abby still lurked. Even the new Abby had trouble accepting the strength of Jake's sexual interest in her. She was glad when his eyes swung back on to the road.

'No more talk now,' he said abruptly. 'I have to concentrate or I really will lose my licence.'

Abby didn't mind not talking. That way she could get back to living in the moment. She certainly didn't want to discuss her marriage any more, because inevitably it made her remember her miscarriages and the pain associated with them.

Maybe Wayne's death was a blessing in disguise, Abby decided. Because she knew she could not bear to ever lose another baby. That was why she didn't want to marry again. That was why she couldn't. But of course she could never tell Jake that. He would think she was emotionally damaged. Which, admittedly, she was. She'd always wanted children—wanted to give them the kind of secure and loving upbringing which she'd never had.

Failing to fulfil this most basic human need had been devastating for her. Her last miscarriage had nearly broken her, as had Wayne's tragic death. She'd been dreadfully depressed for months. But eventually she'd begun to recover, finding a resilience and a courage which surprised her.

Signing up with the Housewives For Hire agency had just been the first step in her plan to embrace a different life than that of marriage and children. As soon as she'd got her job with Jake, she'd begun putting that plan in action by saving every cent she could. Even if Jake's wonderful uncle hadn't left her all that money in his will, she would eventually have saved up enough to travel. In the meantime, she would have done a course to help her with her finances. Something in hospitality. A barista course perhaps, and a bar course. There was always work for an attractive girl in pubs and cafés.

And she *was* attractive, Abby conceded, as she smiled at herself in the side mirror of the car. Attractive enough for Jake to consider her girlfriend material. In truth, he seemed well and truly smitten now, enough to consider taking her away on a grand tour with him. Her mind still boggled a bit at that one. Obviously, he genuinely enjoyed her company. It came to Abby that Jake was somewhat jaded with life at the moment, hence his desire to sell his television show and travel overseas. And who better to go with but a female companion for whom he currently had the hots and who would be oh, so impressed by all the places he took her? Which, no doubt, she would be. No use pretending she wouldn't.

But how long before her lack of worldly experience and serious lack of education wasn't quite so appealing? Would it irk him when he couldn't have the same kind of intellectual conversations which he'd had with his very clever uncle and that last newsreader girlfriend who probably had a degree in journalism or communication or whatever degree newsreaders had to have? Female newsreaders weren't just pretty faces these days. They were also smart. Super smart.

Abby realised all of a sudden that silence wasn't good for her. It led to too much negative thinking. She'd come a long way lately in feeling good about herself and she didn't aim to go backwards.

After glancing around, Abby was surprised to realise she actually recognised where she was. On the long avenue which led to the centre of Canberra. She felt sure that soon they would go over a bridge and then past lots of famous buildings before ending up in front of a grassy hill on which stood the houses of parliament—both old and new.

'I remember more of this than I thought I did,' she said as they approached the bridge which crossed Lake Burley Griffin, named after the man who'd designed the city of Canberra. Abby recalled vaguely that he was an American architect who had won some sort of competition to have the honour, but she didn't say so in case she was wrong.

'Well, the layout of Canberra is very memorable,' Jake remarked. 'And quite beautiful.'

'Yes, it is,' Abby said as she gazed at the expanse of lovely blue water they were crossing. 'It was a marvellous idea to put a lake in the middle of the city.'

'Did you know you can go for a balloon ride over the city?'

'No, I didn't. But no, thank you. A balloon ride would scare the life out of me.'

'You only live once, Abby.'

'I'd still prefer to keep my feet on the ground, thank you very much.'

He threw her a questioning glance. 'Does that attitude apply to planes as well? Because, if it does, it's going to be a slow boat ride around the world next year.'

'No. I'm prepared to fly, but only on a very reliable airline, one with an impeccable record for safety.'

Jake smiled. 'I wouldn't dream of letting you fly any other way. You're too precious to me for that. Now, I think we'll whip into this car park over here. It's only a short walk to the National Gallery, where there is a very nice café.'

Less than one minute later, Jake had zapped into an empty space in the underground car park, a dumbstruck Abby still not having recovered from his remark about her being too precious to him. She wondered if he really meant it or if he said that kind of thing to all his girlfriends. Whatever, it had done things to her insides which were perturbing. She didn't want to fall in love with Jake, but it seemed a futile wish if just a few words could send her into such a whirl.

'Don't do that,' he said when she went to open her own door. 'Let me do it for you.'

He jumped out from behind the wheel and strode round the bonnet of the Ferrari with a few long strides, opening the passenger door with a masterful flourish and holding out his hand to her.

Abby almost told him that he didn't have to play the gentleman with her. He hadn't done this when he'd taken her car shopping. Or at any other time today. Though she hadn't exactly given him the opportunity, had she? This morning she'd driven her own car home, with Jake following in the Ferrari. Then, after she'd changed outfits, she'd hurried out of the house and practically dived into the passenger seat before any of the neighbours saw her. Jake had rolled his eyes at her at the time but she hadn't twigged to why.

'Do you treat all your girlfriends like this?' she asked him as she placed her hand in his.

His fingers closed tightly around hers as he helped her out of the low-slung seat. 'Only when the woman deserves it. Which you do, my lovely Abby. You deserve the best of everything.'

'Wow,' she said. 'But really, Jake, you don't have to overdo the compliments. Trust me when I say I'm already a sure thing tonight.'

He laughed, then pulled her into his arms. 'Goodness, but I adore you!'

Abby stared up into his glittering blue eyes and thought that maybe he did. For the moment. But the moment was all that she could rely on. History invariably repeated itself and Jake's history with women was not good.

Abby pushed aside this painful thought, telling herself firmly that she wasn't going to worry about the future. She was going to live for the moment. And this moment felt quite wonderful.

'As much as I would like you to kiss me right now,' she said, 'I am in desperate need of the ladies' room. And then something to eat.'

CHAPTER TWENTY-FOUR

As Jake took the last swallow of his coffee he began wondering how best to spend the afternoon. He had no intention of arriving at the hotel he'd booked till after five, well aware that he wouldn't be able to keep his hands off Abby once they were alone. He didn't want this weekend to be nothing but a sex-fest. He wanted to *show* Abby that he enjoyed her company out of bed as well as in. Hopefully, that would allay her fears that he would quickly get bored with her.

'Did you visit this place when you came down with your school?' he asked. 'Not this café. The National Gallery itself.'

'No, I don't think so. We weren't here all that long. Only two days. We drove down one morning and had lunch in a park somewhere. Then in the afternoon we visited both parliament houses. Then they drove us out to a kind of tourist park for the night. The next day they brought us back in here to visit a science centre. Can't remember what it was called. It started with a Q.'

'Questacon,' he said. 'It's not far from here. I went there once. Great place.'

Abby rolled her eyes. 'For you maybe. I found it boring.'

'Well, you won't find the National Gallery boring. The art in here is fabulous. Not just paintings either, but sculptures as well.'

Abby looked a bit worried. 'I don't know all that much about art.'

'That's probably better then. You won't have any preconceived ideas. Promise me you won't say you like something just because it's in here, okay? Some of the purchases have been very controversial over the years. Have you ever heard of *Blue Poles*?'

'It rings a vague bell,' she replied, frowning.

'It's a very famous painting by an American artist, Jackson Pollock. It was bought by this gallery in 1972 for one point three million. They had to get special permission from the Prime Minister at the time to spend that much money. Caused a massive stir. Still, it's reputed to be worth up to twenty million now so I guess it was a good investment after all. Come on. I'll take you to see it,' he said, standing up and reaching for her hand.

'It's huge!' was Abby's first comment when she stood in front of the painting, which measured approximately two by five metres.

'It certainly is.'

'The artist must have had to stand on a ladder to paint the top bits.'

'Actually, he did it whilst it was lying flat on the floor. But that's all beside the point. Do you *like* it?'

Abby scrunched up her face as she stepped back and stared at it for a long moment. 'I can't make up my mind if it's brilliant or an Emperor's New Clothes piece of rubbish.'

Jake had to smile. Only Abby would dare to question what was considered to be Jackson Pollock's best work.

'No, no, I take that back,' she said after a few more seconds of narrow-eyed scrutiny. 'It's definitely one of those paintings that grows on you. But you could hardly hang it in your living room, could you?'

'True,' Jake said, trying not to laugh. But she was such a delight. And so natural, her opinions untainted by the one-eyed opinions of art critics and pseudo intellectuals.

'I certainly wouldn't pay twenty million for it,' she added.

'Me neither,' a male voice said from just behind them.

Jake recognised that voice. Instantly.

He spun round. 'Tony Green, you old devil! Fancy running into you here.'

Abby was astonished when Jake enfolded a tall, skinny, darkly bearded man in a big bear hug.

'I thought you weren't ever coming back to Australia,' Jake added as the man hugged him back. When at last they pulled apart they both had boyish grins on their happy faces.

'Neither were you, if I recall,' the bearded man said. 'Till a bullet changed your mind.'

Abby sucked in sharply at this news, but Jake just shrugged. 'I was about ready to come home, Tony. I'd had enough. Now, before we go and have a drink together and catch up on old times, I think I should make some introductions.' He turned back to Abby and took her by the hand again. 'Abby, this is Tony Green, the most fearless cameraman money can buy. But also just a tad dangerous to work with.'

Tony laughed. '*You* ought to talk. This man's a maniac. I told him he was crazy to go into that particular village that day, but he wouldn't take any notice. Said he'd come to help rescue some girls who'd been kidnapped by a gang of rebels and he was going to free them, come hell or high water. He just wouldn't listen to reason. And guess what? The girls did get rescued but our boy here almost lost his life in the process.'

'Goodness!' Abby exclaimed. 'I had no idea...'

Tony grinned. 'Modest as well as brave. That's our Jake. But also stubborn. Once Jake makes his mind up to do something, nothing will change his mind. But then you probably already know that, since I gather you two are an item.'

'We are,' Jake said, giving Abby's hand a squeeze. 'And I'll have you know I'm not a maniac any longer.'

'Possibly true. I couldn't believe it when I got back to Australia last month and saw you hosting that chat show. I mean, that's not you, mate.'

'It suited me at the time, Tony. And it's my own production. But I've decided to sell it before Christmas. Abby and I are going on a world tour together next year. *Not* to the places *we* went to. To the nice places.'

'Wow. So you two are pretty serious about each other then?'

'You could say that,' Jake replied, and gave Abby's hand another squeeze.

'You *have* changed. Look, as much as I'd like to get a drink and catch up on old times, I can't. I'm meeting someone up at Parliament House in about fifteen minutes. I just popped in here to fill in time till she gets off work.'

'Someone special?' Jake asked.

'Very. We met over the internet. She's the reason I came back to Australia.'

'I see. Well, I hope it works out for you.'

'You too. We should stay in touch.'

'I'm on Facebook,' Jake told him.

'Me too. Have to go, mate. It's been great seeing you again.'

They hugged once more and Tony was gone.

'Well,' said Jake with a sigh, 'fancy that. I honestly never expected to see him again.'

There was so much Abby wanted to ask Jake, the many questions in her head underlining how much she didn't know about him and the job he used to do. But right now, here in this gallery, with people milling around, didn't seem the right place to have such a conversation.

'I don't really want to walk around looking at art, Jake,' she said truthfully. 'Can't we just go to that hotel you booked? Or is it too early?'

Their eyes met, the desire which they'd both put on hold earlier flaring between them.

'And you accused me of corrupting you,' he murmured wryly, then glanced at his watch. 'It's only half past two. Check-in time isn't till three. But I suppose I could call them and play the celebrity card.'

He played the celebrity card, Abby wishing for a few excruciating minutes in Reception that he hadn't. The behaviour of the attractive brunette behind the desk was more than embarrassing. She gushed all over Jake, half flirting with him whilst totally ignoring Abby's presence. By the time Jake steered Abby over to the bank of lifts in the corner, she wasn't sure who she felt sorrier for, herself or Jake.

She sighed as they entered a blessedly empty lift.

'Yes, I know,' he said ruefully. 'But it won't be like that when we're booking into hotels overseas. Over there, I'll be a nobody.'

'I suspect you'll always get special treatment from female staff, Jake,' Abby said a bit tartly. 'You're way too handsome for your own good.'

He smiled at her. 'That's the pot calling the kettle black. I haven't forgotten the way dear old Raoul came on to you, beautiful.'

Abby blinked up at him. 'Are you saying you were jealous of Raoul?'

'Painfully so.'

'Good,' she said, and he laughed.

'I like it when you get stroppy with me. And when you're jealous.'

The lift doors opened on the tenth floor, Jake wasting no time steering Abby along the corridor to their room. Their overnight bags were waiting for them inside, as was a bottle of chilled champagne and a fruit basket, courtesy of the management. The room was what was called superior, with views over the lake, a separate sitting area, a king-sized bed and a spa bath.

Although impressed, Abby wasn't all that interested in any of it. All she wanted by then was for Jake to take her in his arms and kiss her.

'Care for a glass of champagne?' he asked her as he lifted the bottle out of the ice bucket and set about opening it.

Abby winced. How did you tell a man that all you wanted was him?

He glanced over at her then and laughed. 'You should see the look on your face.'

Now she blushed.

'I take it you don't want the champagne just

yet,' he said as he walked slowly across the room to where she was standing beside the bed.

'Do you?' she asked him.

'The only thing I want at the moment, my darling girl,' he said, 'is you.'

He undressed her quickly, without so much as a kiss, not stopping till she was totally naked. Then he left her standing there like that whilst he undressed, his eyes on her all the while. Her own gaze was hot and hungry as she watched him strip off, her need intense before he'd even laid a finger on her. She closed her eyes when he scooped her up and laid her on the bed, gasping when he started stroking her body, first her breasts then her stomach, her thighs, her calves.

'No, no...' she moaned when he spread her legs and used his mouth on her.

But protesting was useless and she splintered apart under his tongue within seconds. Her climax hadn't abated when he rolled her over on to her stomach and started stroking her again. Her back this time, then her buttocks. And between. She writhed beneath his knowing hands, and his wickedly probing fingers. In no time her desire for release became desperate again. Her legs moved invitingly apart, her hips moving restlessly in a circular fashion.

'Not that way, my darling,' he growled, and flipped her back over. 'Not this time. I want to see your eyes when you come. Just give me a sec.'

She groaned at the time he took to don the condom, crying out when he entered her at last, penetrating her with a forceful surge which filled her to the hilt. His own eyes, she noted, were wildly glittering, his breathing ragged. He groaned when she wrapped her legs high around his back, pressing her hips hard up against his.

'Hell on earth, woman,' he ground out. 'Be still or I'll come.'

'I want you to come,' she told him in a wickedly wanton voice as she moved her hips in a slow sensual circle, squeezing him at the same time.

A decidedly crude four-letter word punched from his throat.

Abby didn't swear much herself, but somehow, today, at this moment, it turned her on. 'Yes,' she said with a low moan. 'That's what I want, too. Just do it, Jake. I don't care if I come or not.'

'Bloody hell,' he muttered, then started to move, the veins in his throat standing out as he set up a steady rhythm.

Abby was touched by his efforts to last, but she would have none of it, certain that she would come if he came. She kept squeezing him mercilessly, and rotating her hips, watching with increasing frustration as he tried desperately to maintain control. Desperate herself now, she removed her hands from where they'd been gripping the sheet on either side of her, clamping them onto his buttocks and digging her nails in as she pulled him even deeper into her.

It was the final straw for Jake, tipping him over the edge with a speed and power which Abby found thrilling. He didn't watch her come because his eyes were shut at the time. But come she did, exulting in the way her body matched his, spasm for spasm. They shuddered together for ages till finally they were done, Jake rolling from her and collapsing on to the bed, still gasping and panting. Abby just lay where she was, a very deep languor seeping through her sated body as her breathing calmed and her muscles relaxed. She didn't want to go to sleep, but her mind had other ideas. Five minutes later she was out like a light.

CHAPTER TWENTY-FIVE

JAKE WAS BEYOND words for some considerable time. Frankly, he was somewhat stunned at how he'd lost control of the lovemaking. There he'd been, thinking he would show Abby this weekend what a great lover he was and bingo, he'd come with the speed of a randy teenager. For a girl of limited experience, she seemed to know exactly what to do to drive a man wild.

Jake sighed. So much for not wanting this weekend to be a sex-fest. Suddenly, that was all he could think about. His head turned to where Abby was lying on the bed, her naked body splayed out in the most provocative pose. Unfortunately, she was also sound asleep. But that didn't stop Jake from looking.

Naked, Abby had the sort of body a man could look at for hours, with its delicious combination of slenderness and curves. Her breasts were just the right size. Full but not heavy, her nipples surprisingly large and yes, very responsive. Not pink, they were a dusky brown colour which made them stand out from her rather pale skin. Jake's stomach tightened at the urge to roll over right now and suck them. But he didn't. Though he would, after he'd been to the bathroom. She didn't need to sleep for long. Hell, it was only mid-afternoon. She could sleep later tonight, after he'd run out of steam. And condoms.

Climbing off the bed, Jake walked into the bathroom to attend to the condom. He wished he didn't have to use them.

'I really don't want to take *any* chances, Jake,' she'd reiterated at breakfast today. 'I went through a few nasty moments there last night when I thought I'd forgotten to take my Pill.'

It would have given him more than a *few* nasty moments if she'd become pregnant, Jake accepted. Which meant he would just have to keep on using condoms.

Not that it really mattered. Safe sex was a way of life for him. Still, perhaps after they'd been together for a while, she might tell him not to bother with the condoms any more. He trusted her to take the Pill every day. After all, she seemed just as paranoid about falling pregnant as he was. Meanwhile, he still had almost a dozen condoms left for this weekend, which seemed overly ambitious…but then he walked back into the bedroom and saw that Abby had rolled over and curled up into a foetal position.

Just looking at Abby's peachy bottom started doing things to him which would have been impossible a few minutes earlier.

Jake climbed back on to the bed with a rueful smile on his face.

'Abby, darling,' he crooned, running a single finger up and down her spine. 'You can't go to sleep yet. It's only four o'clock.'

'Go away,' she mumbled. 'Tired.'

Jake smiled as he rose and went back into the bathroom, where he poured some of the provided bath salts into the spa bath he'd noted earlier. After that, he turned on the water, adjusted the temperature, then went to collect the champagne and the fruit basket, the bath fortunately having ledges large enough in each corner to accommodate the ice bucket and two glasses. Once the water was at the right height, he switched off the taps, hid a couple of condoms amongst the fruit then joined Abby on the bed, this time bending his lips to her shoulder.

'Jake calling Abby,' he murmured between kisses. 'Do you hear me, Abby?'

Her eyes fluttered open as her head turned

and gazed up at him with heavy lids. 'You can't possibly want to do it again this soon,' she said sleepily.

'Not right away,' he said. 'I've run us a spa bath. There's room enough for two.'

She blinked, then sat up abruptly, her messy hair falling across her forehead and one eye. 'But I haven't… I've never…'

'What happened to the girl who told me she wanted to experience everything?' he said as he gently pushed her hair back from her eyes. 'Trust me, okay?'

She rolled her eyes at this.

'I've taken some refreshments in there for us to enjoy,' he went on. 'I thought you might be hungry. We can eat and talk at the same time.'

'You want to talk? I thought you wanted sex.'

'Not until you wake up properly.'

Jake kept a straight face as he said this.

But, perversely, Abby took him at his word.

'So what are we going to talk about?' she said even before she'd lowered herself into the warm water.

'Whatever you'd like to talk about,' he replied, temporarily settling back into the opposite end of the bath. 'But first I'll pour us both some champagne.'

Abby wondered as she watched Jake pour the bubbly just how often he'd done this. She wasn't jealous, but she did rather envy his know-how. Did he have any idea how awkward she felt at the moment? How…ignorant?

Not a total fool, however. He hadn't brought her in here to talk. And whilst she did want him to make love to her some more in whatever exotic ways he wanted, there *was* something she wanted to talk to him about whilst she had the chance.

'That man in the gallery, Jake,' she said as he handed her a glass of champagne. 'Tony,' she added after taking a sip.

'What about him?' Jake asked.

'He said you were shot. And I was wondering where.' She hadn't seen any scars on him.

'Africa. Sierra Leone.'

'No, no, I mean where on your body.'

He laughed. 'Here,' he said, and showed her a scar on his inner thigh which was more towards the back than the front. No wonder she hadn't seen it.

'Heavens. You were very lucky.'

'Sure was. A couple of inches either way and I would have lost the family jewels.'

'Which would have been a dreadful shame.'

'My feelings exactly.'

'Still, it was very brave of you to do what you did that day.'

'More stupid than brave.'

'I don't agree. So I suppose that was when you stopped making documentaries?'

'Yep. I had to come home to get proper medical treatment. Then, once I was home, I decided I'd had enough of traipsing around the world. Craig said I'd get tired of it one day and he was right.'

'Then why do you want to go back overseas?'

'Travelling as a tourist is very different from what I was doing, Abby. Have you seen any of the documentaries I made?'

'No.'

'Then don't. They're grim viewing.'

'Then why did you make them?'

He shrugged. 'Initially, I thought it would be great fun, following Craig around and filming the places he went and the things he witnessed. But after a few years I found myself becoming emotionally involved in the injustices I saw. I naively thought that if the problems of the Third World were shoved in the face of the Western World, they might do something to solve at least some of those problems. That was when I became a crusader. But I was deluding myself.

People liked watching my more hard-hitting documentaries. I made a lot of money out of them.
But they didn't inspire much action. There's still
war and poverty and abuse of the worst kind.
Nothing ever changes.'

'But you tried,' Abby said gently. 'All you can
do is try, Jake.'

'You *are* sweet,' he said. 'But could we possibly change the subject?'

Abby was touched by his sensitivity. Clearly,
he wasn't as selfish and self-centred as he liked
to pretend. But then, she'd already known that,
hadn't she, even before she'd heard the good
things Tony had said about him. Look at the way
he'd followed through with his uncle's legacy to
her, even though he hadn't wanted to at first.

A thought suddenly occurred to her.

'Were you telling the truth when you said you
were jealous of Raoul?'

'Jealous? I wanted to tear him limb from limb.'

'But why? I mean…we weren't an item then.'

'Maybe not. But I already wanted you like
crazy.'

She shook her head from side to side. 'I find
that hard to believe.'

'Oh, Abby, Abby, you gorgeous thing, you.'
He sighed and shook his head back at her. 'You

don't understand men very well, do you? Now, drink up your champers, sweet thing. I have an urge to have my wicked way with you. All chit-chat is to cease as of this moment. That is, except for words like, *Yes, Jake. Please, Jake. Don't stop, Jake.*'

She couldn't help it. She laughed.

'Don't you dare laugh at me, you cheeky minx.'

She smiled instead and said, 'Yes, Jake.'

CHAPTER TWENTY-SIX

IT WAS LIGHT when Abby came to consciousness, turning over on to her back and stretching before glancing over at the sleeping male form next to her in the bed. Jake was lying on his side, his back to her, his breathing deep and heavy.

She smiled in memory of Jake's reluctance to let her go to sleep, even when it was obvious he'd exhausted himself making love to her. The only time they'd stopped was first at six-thirty so she could take her Pill and then when he'd ordered room service around eight, a huge seafood platter which they'd devoured together in record time before getting back to devouring each other.

Abby picked up her phone from the bedside table and checked the time, surprised to find that it was after nine. They'd finally gone to sleep around two, so both of them had had a good seven hours of sleep. Still, no need to wake Jake yet, she decided, rising quietly and going to the bathroom. Closing the door behind her, she turned on the light and took a good look at herself in the large mirror.

Not only was her hair a total mess—she really should have put it up before that last shower—but she had faint bruises on her breasts.

'Goodness, Abby,' she said, sounding slightly shocked. 'You look like a woman who's been well and truly ravaged.'

'And didn't you just love it,' she answered herself in a low sexy voice which wasn't at all shocked.

The new Abby realised there was no point in pretending. Given she was unlikely ever to come across a lover like Jake again, she aimed to take full advantage of his erotic skills—plus his gorgeous male body—whilst she had the chance. If she had to have her heart broken by him at some stage in the future, then she was going to enjoy herself in the meantime.

Though how long that meantime lasted was anybody's idea, she accepted with an inevitable lurching of her silly female heart. Okay, so he'd asked her to go overseas with him next year. And he *had* sounded as if he meant it. But that could just have been a wild impulse on his part. He could change his mind tomorrow. Or next week. Or next month. It was only mid November. All she could rely on was today. The present. This moment.

'That's it, kiddo,' she told herself firmly. 'Live for the moment. Now, go wake up old sleepy-head.'

With her body buzzing from wicked resolve, Abby returned to the bedroom and climbed in under the sheet next to a still unconscious Jake. She didn't hesitate, snuggling up to him with her naked front pressed up against his back, her left hand free to travel at will over his body, much the same way as he had done to her in the bath. He stirred slightly the moment her fingers brushed over his nipples, but shot awake with a raw gasp when her hand moved further south.

'You have a beautiful penis,' she murmured. 'Nice and long. And so silky up here.'

He made a strangled sound as she ran her thumb pad over the engorged tip.

'You like that, don't you?' she crooned, another echo of what he'd said to her when he'd teased her at length in the water. 'But you'd rather I do this with my tongue, wouldn't you?'

When he swore she laughed. 'No, not this time, Jake. This time you're going to let me have *my* wicked way with *you.*'

It surprised Abby how in control she felt, her

own needs firmly in check as she set about making *him* lose control. She loved it when he called out her name as he came, blown away by the satisfaction she felt as his whole body shook.

But alongside the satisfaction lay the certainty that she would not feel this way with any other man. The realisation hit suddenly that she loved Jake—loved him in the way she should have loved Wayne, but hadn't. The thought sent tears into her eyes, tears of guilt and regret and true sadness.

The old Abby might have fallen apart at that moment. The new Abby was a far tougher creature. She told herself firmly that she'd gone into this affair with her eyes open and it was a little late to start becoming maudlin. So she gathered her emotions, blinked away the tears and lifted her head.

It was impossible not to look at him. Impossible to stop her emotions suddenly getting the better of her. How awful it was to love someone the way she loved Jake without being able to tell him.

Jake was taken aback when he saw she was on the verge of tears.

'Abby! Darling! What is it? What's wrong?'

'Oh, God,' she cried, then burst into tears.

Stricken with remorse over he knew not what, Jake cuddled her close, searching his mind at the same time for the reason behind her tears.

'Tell me what's wrong,' he said as he cradled her face and rained kisses all over it.

She made a choking sound, closing her eyes at the same time.

'You wanted to do that, didn't you? I didn't ask you. You *wanted* to. And I loved it. Truly I did.'

Still, she said nothing, just buried her face into his shoulder and wept.

'Please don't cry, my darling.'

She opened her still wet eyes then and just stared at him. 'Don't call me that,' she blurted out. 'I'm not your darling.'

Jake didn't know how to respond. Had her husband called her his darling? Was that it?

'What do you want me to call you?'

She closed her eyes again as she shook her head. 'Oh, God. I'm so stupid.'

Jake sighed. He wished he knew what was going on in her head. But he'd never been good at reading women's minds. Females could be complex creatures. Maybe she was hormonal. Maybe her period was due. All he knew was that he hated seeing her upset, her tears calling to something deep inside himself which was impossible to control. His heart actually ached with the need to make her feel better.

'Abby… I hate seeing you like this. I wish you'd tell me what's wrong. I want to be your friend as well as your lover. I want you to feel that you can tell me anything.'

He waited and finally, when she opened her eyes, her expression was calmer. Or was it resigned?

'It's not you,' she said. 'It's me. You haven't done anything wrong. I love what kind of lover you are. I've had more fun with you this weekend than I've had in years.'

Jake pulled a face. Now she made it sound as if he was shallow. Yet he felt anything but shallow when he was making love to her. Perhaps because that was exactly what it was. Making love. Not just having sex. Jake could no longer pretend that he wasn't becoming seriously involved with Abby. He'd avoiding falling in love in the past because he didn't want marriage and children. What Jake hadn't realised was that true love could not be avoided. It just happened. If truth be told, he'd been half in love with Abby from the moment he'd hugged her that awful day, long before she'd stormed past his conscience less than two days ago. Now he was well and truly head over heels.

But of course he couldn't tell her any of that. Not yet. She didn't want him to love her. Not at the moment. Perhaps one day, when the time was right, when he was sure that she returned his feelings, he would declare his love and they would find a way to spend their lives together. Not marriage. Though perhaps a child eventually, if that was what she ever wanted. Jake still wasn't thrilled with the idea of becoming a father but one child might be manageable.

'So why were you crying just now?' he asked.

Abby shrugged. 'This will sound silly but I was feeling guilty that I couldn't give my husband the pleasure that I obviously give you. Wayne deserved better than a wife who didn't really love him.'

'You did love him, Abby,' he reassured her. 'I know you. You wouldn't have married him if you hadn't loved him. Maybe it wasn't a mad passion but it was love all the same. It wasn't your fault that the physical chemistry between you wasn't right. It wasn't his fault, either. But that's all in the past, Abby. You can't change what happened in your marriage and it's a waste of time to beat yourself up over it.'

'You're right,' she said, nodding. 'I can't change anything that's already happened. All we have is the present. I decided earlier today that I want to live in the moment from now on. That's what you do, isn't it?'

'To a degree,' he replied carefully. 'I do make some plans for the future when required.'

'You mean like when going overseas.'

'That's a good example. You can't just show up at the airport and take the first available flight. You need to do things first.'

'Like get a passport,' she said, her eyes looking marginally happier.

'Indeed,' he said, smiling.

'I'll get straight on to that first thing next week. And I might do some more clothes shopping at some stage. I don't want you ever feeling ashamed of me.'

Jake was truly taken aback. 'I would never be ashamed of you.' But it did occur to him that women thought differently to men on matters of fashion.

'You should go clothes shopping with Sophie. She would know exactly what you need. I tell you what; I'll ring and ask her to take you.'

'Oh, no, don't do that. I can't afford the sort of clothes your sister would show me.'

'Yes, you can. I'll give her my credit card. It doesn't have a limit.'

'I can't let you do that!' she exclaimed.

'Why not?'

'Because...because...'

'I'm a very rich man, Abby. I want to do this for you. Please don't say no.'

'I shouldn't let you.'

'Don't be silly. I'll ring her and tell her you need a new wardrobe to cover every occasion. Now, no more objections. I insist. And another thing, you have to ring your sister tonight and tell her about us.'

Abby groaned. 'I really don't want to, Jake.'

'And I don't want to keep on being your secret lover,' he growled. 'I certainly don't intend to spend every date with you wearing sunglasses and a baseball cap. The world is going to find out about us sooner or later, Abby, and there's nothing you can do about that.'

'I know,' she said with a sigh. 'But at least we have today before that happens.'

'Don't you believe it. That receptionist last night was probably on Instagram and Twitter within seconds of our booking in. You can't keep anything a secret these days, not if you're in the public eye. You just have to not care what people think or say. People that don't matter, that is. Family is different.'

'Are you going to tell your family about me?'

Jake smiled. 'I won't have to. Sophie will. But, speaking of family, I want you to join us for our harbour cruise on Christmas Day.'

Dismay filled Abby's face. 'I'm sorry, Jake, but I can't do that. I've already invited Megan and Timmy to spend Christmas Day with me and I would never disappoint them.'

'I see,' he said, thinking he should have known. Olivia would have dumped her family like a shot if he'd asked her to be with him on Christmas Day. But Abby was not Olivia. She was unique. A woman in a million. 'Well, there's no reason why they can't both come on the harbour cruise with all of us,' he said. 'There'll be plenty of room, and plenty of food. And lots of other kids for Timmy to play with.'

'That's incredibly generous of you, Jake, but I'm not sure Megan will want to come.'

'Why's that? Is she shy?'

Abby laughed. 'Not exactly.'

'Look, when you ring her tonight, just ask her.'

'What if she says no?'

'Then I'll ring her and ask her myself. I've

been told I can be very persuasive, when I want to be.'

Abby's expression was pained. 'As long as you don't flirt with her. If you do that, I won't be too happy. She already thinks you're God's gift to women.'

'In that case persuade her to come yourself. Because I don't intend to be without you on Christmas Day. I also want to show you off to my whole family, and that way we can do it all in one go. Far better than having to trot you around to everyone one at a time.'

'You won't tell them about my background, will you? And my teeth!'

'Sorry, sweetheart, they'll already know everything about you by then. Sophie is not renowned for keeping her mouth shut. And why wouldn't you want them to know about your teeth? They look fabulous!'

'I wasn't referring to my new teeth but my old ones.'

'There's nothing shameful about having had problem teeth.'

'Pardon me if I don't think so,' Abby said, rolling away from him on to the bed, her body language indicating she wasn't happy.

'Okay,' he said nonchalantly.

'What?' Stormy green eyes shot his way.

'I'll pardon you. For about ten seconds. You're the one who said you wanted to move on with your life. Well, the first thing for you to do is not be oversensitive about your past. I want to tell my family all about you because I'm serious about you, Abby. I don't want you for a fling. Okay, I might not want marriage but I want you in my life. If you must know, I was attracted to you from the first moment I saw you.'

'You *were*?'

'I certainly was. But I thought you were the sort of woman who would want marriage and children so I kept my distance. Regardless of what you think of me, I am not a compulsive womaniser. I would never target a woman who was emotionally vulnerable, which I thought you were, being a widow. But on Friday night you confirmed that you didn't want to get married again. After that, I decided to hell with resisting temptation any longer. I wanted you like mad by then and decided I was going to have you.'

Only then did Jake realise Abby was looking pole-axed by his confession. He wasn't sure if that meant she was pleased, or sceptical.

'That was why I was jealous of Raoul,' he went on. 'Now, no more of this nonsense. And no more regrets about the past. You're living for the moment, are you not? And the moment calls for two activities. Breakfast first. I don't know about you but I'm starving. Then once we're dressed, fed and out of here I'm going to do something really amazing.'

'And what's that?'

'I'm going to let you drive my car.'

CHAPTER TWENTY-SEVEN

'I CAN'T BELIEVE IT,' Megan said for the umpteenth time since Abby had called her that Sunday night.

Abby sighed. 'I don't know why you keep saying that. You were the one who warned me Jake might come on to me if I smartened myself up.'

'It's not that I don't believe he fancies you; it's all the sex! I always thought you were frigid.'

'Well, I'm obviously not.'

'Obviously. At least, not with lover boy. But then, he's had a lot of practice seducing women.'

'Jake did not seduce me, Megan. I was with him all the way.'

'Honestly?'

'Honestly.'

'Wow.'

'He's asked me to go overseas with him next year.'

'You have to be kidding me.'

'I kid you not. I'm applying for my passport

this week. Apparently, it takes a few weeks to get it.'

'This is insane, Abby. You do know that, don't you? I mean…it won't last. Men like Jake…they don't do for ever.'

'I'm well aware of that, Megan. He was nothing if not brutally honest with me on that score. No marriage and no children. But he claims he does want a relationship with me, not just a fling. So I am going to go overseas with him and nothing you say is going to stop me.'

'Oh, God, you've fallen in love with the bastard, haven't you?'

Abby sighed again. 'Jake is not a bastard, Megan. He's a very nice man. A gentleman, in fact. And yes, I've fallen in love with him. But not to worry. I've already come to terms with my feelings. I know I'm going to be hurt at some time in the future but I've decided not to worry about the future for a while. Or the past. I'm living for the here and now. Jake likes me. A lot. And he wants me. A lot. I won't give that up just because it might end badly one day.'

'I've never heard you talk like this, Abby. You sound so sure. And so mature.'

'I've grown up a bit since Wayne died.'

'He wasn't right for you,' Megan said gently, bringing a lump to Abby's throat.

'I can see that now,' Abby agreed. 'I talked with Jake about my marriage and he said I had to let it go. That it was past history.'

'He's right. But surely you didn't tell Jake everything, did you? I mean I know how you hate talking about your miscarriages.'

Abby's heart immediately squeezed tight in her chest. 'No, I didn't tell him about them. He thinks we were trying for a baby but it just didn't happen. It was more my relationship with Wayne I talked about. I told Jake I didn't want to get married again.'

'When did you say that?'

'I'm not sure. Some time recently. It might have been the day he took me car shopping.'

'After which he decided it was safe to seduce you,' came Megan's dry remark.

Abby rolled her eyes. 'Whatever.' Abby hadn't told Megan about Jake's declaration that he'd had the hots for her from the day he hired her. Mostly because Megan was too cynical to believe that. But, surprisingly, Abby did. For she could find no reason for Jake to lie to her. Not that it would change the ultimate outcome of their relationship. It gave Abby a real thrill to think she'd captured his interest but he'd cared enough about her emotional well-being not to pursue her at the time.

'I bet you'd marry Jake in a shot if he asked you to.'

'He isn't going to, Megan. He has, however, asked me to spend Christmas Day with him and his extended family on a harbour cruise.'

'Wow. He must be pretty serious about you then, if he wants you to meet his mum and dad.'

'He's only got a mum. His dad's dead. But he also has two brothers and three sisters, four of whom are married with children.'

'Good grief, I hope it's a big boat.'

'Very big, he said. Which is why you and Timmy are invited as well.'

'What? You're kidding! This is just so out there. I'm going on a harbour cruise with Jake Sanderson and his family? Golly, I'll have to go on a diet straight away. And buy something new to wear.'

'Speaking of new clothes, I'm going clothes shopping with Jake's sister some time this week. Jake insisted on buying me a whole new wardrobe.'

'Seriously? A whole new wardrobe?'

'Yes. And before you make any smart cracks

about me being a kept woman, how about I get her to pick out something for you at the same time? I know your size and she'll choose something really stylish, since she's a stylist.'

Megan laughed. 'You're worried I'm going to turn up in something cheap and trashy, aren't you?'

'Not at all!' Abby exclaimed.

'You're such a bad liar. But not bad at keeping secrets, it turns out. There I was, trying to ring you all weekend and getting really mad, thinking that you'd accidentally turned off your phone. And now I find out that you did it on purpose so that you and your boss could bonk away like a pair of bloody rabbits.'

'You have such a delicate turn of phrase.'

'Gee, Abby. Ever since you started reading all those fancy books you seem different.'

'Different? How?'

'Oh, you know. Like you had some toffee-nosed education. Don't forget your roots, girl. You're a Westie and there's nothing you can do to change that.'

'I'm not trying to change that. I know exactly where I came from. But there's nothing wrong with trying to better myself. Even if my affair with Jake hadn't happened, I would have been going to night school next year, as well as saving up to travel all by myself.'

'But Jake has happened, so now you'll drop all those plans. Just don't forget that when *he* drops *you* you're going to lose your job as well. Have you thought of that?'

'It's crossed my mind. But like I said, I'm not going to worry about the future too much, Megan. I'm going to live for the moment.'

'That's because you're madly in love at the moment.'

'You can't talk me out of this, Megan. Now, I'm getting off this phone and going to bed. I've had a very tiring weekend.'

'Yeah, so I heard. I still can't believe it. Did you two do anything else this weekend except have wild sex?'

'I never said it was wild.'

'Yeah, right. Pull the other leg. I'll bet lover boy did more to you in one weekend than Wayne did in five frigging years.'

'You could be right there.'

'Ooh, do tell!'

'Absolutely not. I'm off to bed. Goodnight, Megan.'

Abby shook her head as she terminated the call then turned off her phone. She didn't have a landline so her sister and her curiosity would have to wait. Megan might want her to give a blow-by-blow account of her various sexual escapades but Abby was not that kind of girl. She was a very private person. And so was Jake, in his own way. She could see he didn't overly like his celebrity status any more than she did.

Abby got herself ready for bed, since she actually was *very* tired. Which was just as well. She didn't want to lie in bed and start overthinking everything. There was a time for deep and meaningful thinking, and it wasn't now. Now was the time for sleep.

Abby was settling herself down into sleep mode when all of a sudden she remembered that Jake had asked her to call him and tell her how things went with Megan. Sitting up in bed abruptly, she reached for her phone, instantly energised by the thought of talking to Jake. He answered on the second ring.

'I was beginning to think you weren't going to call me,' he said.

'I'm sorry, Jake. I forgot.'

'That's not very flattering, I must say. A couple of hours out of my sight and you forget me.'

Abby knew he wasn't really angry. She could hear the teasing note in his voice. 'You're not

going to be one of those boyfriends, are you?'
she teased back.

'And what kind is that?'

'The obsessive kind.'

'That depends on whether you're going to be
one of those girlfriends.'

'And what kind is that?'

'The ones who drive men insane because they
don't ring when they say they're going to.'

'I said I was sorry.'

'You also said you forgot.'

'I dare say you're not used to being forgotten.'

'Not often. But all this is beside the point. Did
you tell your sister about us?'

'Yes.'

'And?'

'She wasn't shocked that we're sleeping together, but she's worried that I'm going to lose
my job when we eventually break up.'

'Who says we'll eventually break up?'

'It seems likely, given your history with
women.'

'I'm not as fickle as the tabloids make out.'

'I know that. But, in any case, I'm not worried.
I can always get another job, provided you give
me a good reference.'

'I'm not sure I like that sister of yours. She sounds like trouble.'

'She's only looking after my best interests.'

'And I'm not?'

'Don't go getting all huffy, Jake. Why do you think I didn't want to ring her? But you insisted. Sometimes she rattles me with her cynicism but this time I didn't take notice of anything she said, which rather pleased me. I want to be with you, Jake, and nothing that Megan or anyone else says is going to change my mind.'

'You've no idea how glad I am to hear that. Because I want to be with you too. And not for just a few weeks, or a few months. I have a feeling this relationship might go the whole nine yards.'

Abby sucked in sharply. 'And what does that mean?'

'Now, don't *you* go getting all huffy. I'm not talking marriage. But I am talking about living together, as of tomorrow.'

'Tomorrow?'

'Too soon for you?'

Abby tried not to lose her head. She might be madly in love with Jake but she wasn't about to let him run every aspect of her life.

'A little,' she said. 'How about we wait till after Christmas?'

'But that's over five weeks away!'

'That's hardly a lifetime.'

'So you're knocking me back.'

'I'd like us to just date for a while before taking such a big step.'

'But you've already agreed to go away with me next year,' Jake argued.

'Yes, but that's just a holiday, not real life.'

'Not real life,' he echoed, clearly taken aback.

'Jake, could we not get into this right now? I'm tired and I want to go to sleep. We can talk about this tomorrow.'

Jake could not believe that Abby was giving him the brush-off. He hadn't been on the receiving end of that before. He almost blurted out that he loved her but he held his tongue just in time.

'Fair enough,' he said. 'Till tomorrow then. Goodnight.'

'Goodnight, Jake. And thank you again, for such a wonderful weekend.'

Jake kept the dead phone clamped to his ear for ages whilst he tried to work out exactly what he was feeling. Frustration, mainly. Not sexual frustration—frustration that for the first time in his life he wanted more from a relationship than the woman did. Not only did he want Abby to move in with him, he wanted her to love him the way he loved her. But she didn't want to fall in love. She wanted fun and games, with a fancy holiday overseas thrown in for good measure.

'Not real life,' he growled when he finally threw his phone down. He'd show her real life. He'd take her to places in Asia and Africa where real life meant crippling poverty and appalling cruelty, with no hope for the future.

But no sooner had these vengeful thoughts entered his head than Jake realised he would never do anything so contemptible. Abby deserved better than to be on the receiving end of that kind of behaviour. She deserved the very best this world had to offer. He would take her to large vibrant cities like London and Paris, Tokyo and New York. And then there were the magnificent rivers. He'd take her cruising down the Seine, and the Rhine, and the Danube. Maybe even the Nile, if Egypt got its act together.

Jake's good humour returned as he thought about their trip next year. It would be incredible. The trip of a lifetime, for both of them. And who knew, by the time they returned Abby might care about him enough to move in with him permanently. She might even love him.

He wasn't that unlovable, was he?

CHAPTER TWENTY-EIGHT

ABBY HAD ALWAYS liked Jake's house, sometimes fantasising in her head as she'd cleaned it that if she ever had a spare couple of million dollars she would buy herself such a house. She loved the white walls and the polished wooden floors, the high ceilings and the unfussy furniture. She especially loved the sparkling white kitchen and bathrooms.

But as she cleaned Jake's house that Monday morning it wasn't buying such a house she began fantasising about, but living here. Which of course was no longer a wild fantasy but a fact, *if* she changed her mind and moved in, the way Jake wanted her to.

She was tempted. She wouldn't have been human if she wasn't tempted. But as much as Abby had resolved to live in the moment, common sense demanded she not ignore what would happen if she gave in to Jake's suggestion. Before she knew it she would stop being a Housewife For

Hire, but a housewife for real. She'd start thinking of this house as her home and Jake her de facto husband. She'd start cooking for him and caring for him and, yes, loving him with all her heart and soul. Inevitably, the day would come when she'd blurt out how much she loved him.

And that would be the beginning of the end.

Far better, she decided as she worked her way steadily through the upstairs rooms, that she stay strong and not do what Jake wanted. Except in the bedroom, that was. She was not foolish enough to think she wouldn't do whatever he wanted there. Already, she missed his lovemaking, waking this morning with a wave of desire so powerful that it had taken all of her willpower not to ring him on the spot and beg him to come home early from work.

Fortunately, she'd got a grip in time and plunged herself into the shower instead. But her heart had leapt when her phone rang as she exited the bathroom.

It was Jake.

'Hi,' he'd said in that lovely voice of his. 'Sleep well?'

'Like the dead. And you?'

'So-so. I would have slept better if you'd been with me. Which brings me to the point of this early morning call. I understand that you don't want to live with me twenty-four-seven, but most girlfriends sleep over occasionally.'

Abby resisted telling him that she *had* noticed that.

'I probably will,' she'd said carefully. 'But only after we've been out on a date.'

'I see. In that case I'll just have to ask you out every night.'

'I wouldn't want to go out every night, Jake. I do have other things I have to do, and a sister I like to visit.'

'Fair enough. What about tonight?'

She'd wanted to say yes. Desperately so. Abby knew, however, that she had to maintain some control over this relationship or she'd be lost for ever.

'I don't think so, Jake. I noticed this morning that my place needs some attention. If I don't water the garden soon, all my plants will die. We haven't had rain for ages.'

'The weather forecast predicts a storm this afternoon,' he'd pointed out, his voice on the stormy side itself.

'I never listen to weather forecasts.'

'Don't you watch morning television?'

'I don't watch much television these days.' She used to watch it non-stop when she was a stay-at-home wife with no children and nothing much to do. She still watched the occasional movie but on the whole Abby now preferred to read.

'Have you ever watched my show?'

'Once or twice.'

'And?'

'You're very good at what you do.'

'Sophie thinks it's lightweight. And it is. Which is also why it's so popular, and why I'm going to get oodles of money for it.'

'You're definitely going to sell?'

'I've already put the sale in motion. It will take a couple of weeks to finalise things, though. Meanwhile, I have to do the show and keep the ratings up.'

'Right. Maybe I'll watch it today. Tell you what I think of your performance.'

Jake laughed. 'While I've got you on the phone, Sophie is going to ring you today. I told her all about me wanting her to help you with your new wardrobe and she wants to line up a date.'

Abby sighed. 'Do I really have to buy a whole new wardrobe?'

'Why can't you be like other women, Abby? Most of them would be over the moon at getting a whole new wardrobe, especially one chosen by one of Sydney's top stylists.'

'I guess I would like it better if I could pay for it myself. I have the money. Twenty-five thousand dollars, remember?'

'That's not for clothes. That's for travel. Not that I expect you to pay for anything when you're with me. Think of that money as your emergency fund. For later in your life. Or for when you tire of me and want to go your own way.'

Abby knew she would never get tired of Jake. She loved the man. But she could hardly say so. 'If you insist.'

'I insist. I'll be home early so don't rush off till I get there. I have a surprise for you.'

'What kind of surprise?'

'If I told you that then it wouldn't be a surprise.'

'You're a terrible tease, Jake Sanderson.'

'Takes one to know one. See you around about three.'

It wasn't even close to three, Abby thought as she started cleaning Jake's kitchen later that morning. It was only eleven-thirty. But already her body was humming with anticipation. Not just because of his promised surprise but because she wanted to see him, wanted to kiss him, wanted to make love to him, and vice versa.

In the end, she turned on the television at noon

and watched his show, just so that she could feast her eyes on his handsome face and those sexy blue eyes. After it was over, she could hardly remember the content, her mind filling with images of what they'd done together over the weekend and what they might do in the future. No, not the future. Today. This afternoon. As soon as he got home. She could not wait till they went on some stupid date; her need was too strong for that.

Abby was feverishly cleaning the kitchen counter tops when her phone rang again. But it wasn't Jake. It was his sister, Sophie, who was in a rush and quickly told Abby when and where to meet her the following day before apologising and then dashing off before Abby could object to anything.

Like sister like brother, she thought.

By five to three that afternoon, Abby was in quite a state, her body at war with her mind. To throw herself at Jake as soon as he walked in the door would undo all the groundwork she'd laid down to keep some control over her life. But oh, how she wanted him.

The sound of his key in the front door brought a cry to her lips followed by an abrupt stiffening of her spine. *Be strong, Abby! And, above all, be cool.*

He strode into the kitchen, still dressed in the superb suit he'd worn on his show.

'Hi there,' she said, her smile feeling a tad forced. 'Want me to put on some coffee for you?'

'Not particularly,' he replied as he swept across the kitchen and pulled her into his arms.

'Coffee is the last thing on my mind at the moment,' he ground out as his head descended.

'Could I tempt you into sleeping over tonight?' Jake asked when his mouth finally lifted from hers, his hands remaining clamped over her shoulders. 'After I take you out to dinner, of course.'

Abby took a couple of seconds to get her head together, which wasn't easy considering it was totally scrambled.

'I can't stay the whole night,' she said with dismay in her voice. 'Your sister rang and she's arranged to take me shopping all day tomorrow. Which means I have to go home some time tonight and do all sorts of girl things so that I look my best.'

'Fair enough,' Jake said, then kissed her some more.

'What about my surprise?' she asked when he finally gave her a breather.

Jake smiled. 'I almost forgot about that. Look, it's nothing sparkly or expensive. I suspect you don't want to be that kind of girlfriend. It's just a fun present.' And out of his suit pocket he brought a packet of condoms, each one with a different fruit flavour. 'I thought, since we have to use condoms, then we should at least make things interesting.'

Abby had to smile. 'Where on earth did you buy them? Over the internet?'

'Nope. I did a segment on condoms one day on my show and these were given to me as samples. I've had them in a drawer in my dressing room for months.'

Abby liked that he hadn't used them on any of his other girlfriends. 'Such interesting flavours,' she said as she read the list on the packet. 'I like the sound of pineapple and coconut. And, of course, passion fruit. Blood orange sounds dangerous.'

'In that case, we'll try that one first,' he said as he shoved the condom packet in his pocket then bent to scoop her up into his arms.

'Come on,' he said. 'Let's go have some fun.'

CHAPTER TWENTY-NINE

'NO, NOT THAT one,' Sophie said when Abby came out of the dressing room in a black and white spotted dress that she herself had chosen. 'It makes you look too busty. When a girl is as well endowed as you, Abby, she should never wear dresses which come right up to the neck. You should mainly stick to lower necklines, not to mention block colours. You can get away with some patterned materials but only if the design is delicate and not overpowering. That dress you wore last Friday night looked good on you because the pattern wasn't too big, or bright. And the dress had a V neckline, if you recall.'

Abby sighed. 'There's a lot more to choosing the right wardrobe than I ever imagined. It's also very tiring.' They'd been at it all day, only stopping for a light lunch. Admittedly, they'd bought heaps, Sophie waving aside any protest from Abby, claiming she'd been given instructions from Jake that there was to be no expense spared. Abby was to have a full wardrobe suitable for travelling, and which catered for every occasion and season.

Abby had stopped looking at the price tags after a while, but she knew the clothes had to be costing a small fortune, Sophie taking her into several expensive-looking boutiques as well as those floors in the big city department stores which carried the designer ranges. Jake's sister got special treatment everywhere she went, the sales people obviously knowing her well. They didn't even have to carry their purchases around, the various shops agreeing to deliver everything they bought—free of charge.

Whilst Abby felt somewhat overwhelmed by the experience, she suspected she could quickly get used to being treated with such consideration and deference. She could also get used to wearing the kind of clothes which fitted perfectly and looked fantastic. Ignoring any qualms that she was fast becoming a kept woman, Abby resolved to enjoy the experience. After all, Jake could afford it; Sophie told her over coffee just how much he'd inherited from his uncle. Not that she'd sounded jealous. Apparently, Sophie had received a substantial cash legacy, as had all her brothers and sisters; her mother as well.

'Come on,' she said to Abby. 'Get that dress off and we'll call it quits for today. Tomorrow I'll take you shopping for shoes and handbags and underwear.'

'Underwear?' Abby exclaimed.

'Got to have the right underwear, Abby. It can make all the difference to the way a garment looks. Same with the shoes. And then, of course, there's the jewellery.'

'No,' Abby protested at last. 'No jewellery.'

'But...'

'No buts. And no jewellery. I've gone along with this wardrobe business because I don't want to embarrass Jake by not being dressed correctly. But I am his girlfriend, Sophie, not his mistress. So I'd like to keep the underwear and the accessories to a minimum, if you don't mind. I'm not broke. Once I know what I should be buying I can get some of these things myself. I appreciate your help, I really do. But enough is enough!'

'Wow. You can be really forceful when you want to be.'

Abby realised with some surprise that that was true. But forcefulness was a fairly recent trait.

'I've had to learn to be forceful with Jake,' she said. 'He's way too used to getting his own way with women.'

Sophie grinned. 'You could be right there.'

'Did he tell you he asked me to move in with him?'

'No!' Sophie exclaimed, stunned. 'Now that's a first.'

'Oh, dear. Maybe I shouldn't have mentioned it.'

'Why not? Am I right in presuming you said no?'

'Yes, I did. For now, at least.'

'Good for you. Make the devil wait.'

'He might not ask me again,' Abby said with a frown.

Sophie smiled. 'I think he will. Now, why don't you put on those sexy blue jeans you had on earlier? I'll find you a white shirt to go with them, and some little black pumps. Then we'll go down to Café Sydney for some drinks before dinner. I'll text Jake to meet us there instead of going home.'

'No, please don't do that,' Abby said straight away. 'I got a text from Jake earlier today saying that he has a meeting with the man who's buying his show and he's sure to have to take him to dinner. Look, I honestly think I should just go home. I'm wrecked. I wouldn't mind a coffee first, though.'

She didn't want to tell Sophie that she could feel a headache coming on. She really needed to sit down for a while and take a couple of pain-killers before it developed into a migraine.

Unfortunately, by the time they got out of the department store and into a café, Abby was see-ing circles in front of her eyes. Fortunately, the table they were shown to had a bottle of water already on the table with two clean glasses. Abby poured herself a glass immediately then dived into the inner zipped section of her hand-bag where she kept her painkillers. It was also where she always put her Pills if she was going to be away from home in the evening, like last Friday night.

The sight of her strip of Pills made Abby catch her breath. There was one more than there should have been. *What on earth...?*

Instantly alarmed, she checked the strip again.

'What's the matter?' Sophie asked. 'What have you lost?'

Abby groaned. She hadn't lost anything, ex-cept perhaps her mind. For she knew immedi-ately what must have happened. She'd forgotten to take the Pill on the night of the dinner party, just the way she'd feared. And then in the panic of the moment she had miscounted.

Her head spun at the thought of all the unsafe sex she'd had that same night. Just the *possibility* that she might have fallen pregnant sent her stomach swirling and her breathing haywire.

'Abby, what's wrong?' Sophie asked, alarmed.

'I think I'm going to be sick,' she choked out, leaping up and rushing for the Ladies, where she dry retched into the toilet. Afraid that she was going to faint, she sank down on to the tiled toilet floor, pale-faced and panting.

Sophie didn't know what to do. Abby looked dreadful. It reminded her of how her father had looked when he'd had his heart attack. Though surely Abby was too young to have a heart attack.

'Do you have any pains in your chest?' she asked frantically.

When Abby nodded, Sophie didn't hesitate. She called for an ambulance. Ten minutes later, paramedics were checking Abby over, taking her blood pressure and asking her questions. In the end, they declared that she wasn't having a heart attack but a panic attack, which sometimes had similar symptoms to a coronary. They administered a sedative, both for her nausea and her nerves, then suggested Sophie take her straight home. Before they left, one of the paramedics quietly told Sophie to encourage her friend to see a therapist to discover the cause of such a severe panic attack.

Within no time they were in a taxi heading for Balmain, Sophie overriding Abby's request to go to her own home, saying that she wasn't taking her anywhere she would be alone. Then she rang Jake and explained the situation. Not that she could really *explain* the situation.

'A *panic* attack?' Jake exclaimed, sounding both shocked and puzzled. 'What in hell happened to give her a panic attack?'

'Honestly, Jake, I don't know. She was looking for something in her handbag when she suddenly went a ghastly colour. Then she bolted for the Ladies. Look, I suggest you make your excuses and catch a ferry home. I dare say we'll be at your place before you are, even though this is the long way around. I'll put Abby to bed in the downstairs guest room. She's almost asleep now. The ambulance guys gave her something to calm her down.'

'I wish I knew what upset her in the first place.'

'Me too. We'll put our heads together when you get home.'

'I'm on my way.'

'Good.' She clicked off then dropped her phone in her own handbag.

'You shouldn't have called him,' Abby mumbled from where she was half sitting, half lying in the corner of the back seat.

'Are you kidding me? Jake would have had my guts for garters if I hadn't. He loves you, Abby,' Sophie said, not because Jake had confessed as much to her but because she knew her brother better than anyone. No way would he have asked Abby to live with him if he didn't love her.

Abby shook her head from side to side. 'No, he doesn't.'

'Oh, yes, he does,' Sophie insisted, wondering if this was part of Abby's problem—the fact that Jake was asking a lot of her without telling her that he loved her. She would have to speak to him about that.

'But let's not worry about that right now,' Sophie went on, and gently pulled Abby over towards her, putting an arm around her shoulders and cradling her head against her chest. 'All you need to do at the moment is rest.'

When a deeply emotional shudder rippled through Abby's body, Sophie wanted to weep. She wasn't the most empathetic of people, but there was something about Abby which touched her. Sophie could see that she'd touched Jake too, more than anyone else ever had. She had no doubt that he loved her. Of course, it was highly possible her anti-commitment bachelor brother didn't know that he'd fallen in love at long last. Maybe she should tell him. As soon as he got home—*before* he went in to talk to Abby.

His blue eyes stormed at her across the kitchen. 'You're not telling me anything I don't already know, Sophie. I realised over the weekend that I was in love with her.'

'Then why haven't you told her?'

'Perhaps because she doesn't want *any* man to love her at the moment, Miss Smarty-Pants. You heard what she said last Friday night. She doesn't want to get married again. If you don't mind, I would like to go in and talk to Abby and see if I can find out what upset her.'

'She might be asleep,' Sophie called after him as he strode from the room.

She wasn't. She was just lying there in the bed, on her back, her hands crossed over her chest, her eyes fixed on the ceiling. Jake watched her from the doorway for a long moment, his heart going out to her, his ego troubled by the thought that he might not be able to fix whatever it was that had distressed her so much. When he finally walked into the room, she turned her head to look at him, her face bleak but worryingly blank.

'Sophie shouldn't have interrupted your meeting,' she said in a dull voice. 'Or brought me here. I would have preferred to go home but she insisted and I was too weak to argue with her.'

Jake sat down on the side of the bed and picked up one of Abby's hands. It was alarmingly cold.

'She did the right thing,' he said as he gently rubbed her hand with both of his. 'You had a nasty turn, from what I've been told. A severe panic attack, according to the paramedics.'

'Yes,' was all Abby said before she turned her eyes away to stare up at the ceiling again.

Jake hated seeing her like this. So sad. *Too* sad.

'Do you know what caused it?' he asked softly.

'Oh, yes,' she said with a strange sigh.

Jake's hands stilled on her. 'What?'

'The Pill in my handbag,' she answered, still without looking at him. 'I miscounted, which means I didn't take my Pill last Friday night after all. Which also means that I could be pregnant.'

Jake tried to make sense of her rather confused confession but failed, so he just cut to the chase, which was that it *was* possible she'd fallen pregnant last Friday night since they'd had heaps of unsafe sex. He could understand that this would upset her, but not to the extent of having a panic attack. He was definitely missing a piece of the puzzle here.

'You'd have to be unlucky to fall pregnant on one slip-up, Abby,' he pointed out.

She laughed. A short dry laugh which worried the life out of him.

'That's me,' she said. 'Unlucky. Especially when it comes to babies.'

He recalled her saying that she'd tried for a baby during her marriage but it hadn't happened. Which should have reassured her, in a way. Obviously, she didn't fall pregnant easily.

'It's not the end of the world if you did have a baby, is it?'

Again that odd laugh.

'You don't *have* to have a baby these days, Abby,' Jake continued gently. 'Terminations are legal and not dangerous.' Yet even as the words came out of his mouth Jake knew he wouldn't want her to terminate *their* baby. It shocked Jake to discover that he wasn't unhappy with the idea of Abby having his child.

Not Abby, though. She obviously found the idea devastating.

Her eyes flashed his way, eyes full of sudden

fury and hurt. 'I should have known that was what you'd suggest. But you don't have to worry about arranging a termination for me, Jake. I'm the original baby terminator. Put a baby in me and it's lucky to last three months. Do you know what it's like to lose three babies, Jake? No, how could you? You don't want children, anyway. But I did. Once upon a time. More than anything I wanted to make my own family where the mummy and daddy truly loved each other as well as their children. Wayne did, too. He'd been a foster child, did I mention that? My parents were pretty rotten but his were even worse. Oh, God,' she sobbed, her hands lifting to cover her face. 'I failed him on all counts, didn't I?'

When Jake saw the tears seeping out from under her fingers he felt like weeping himself. But at least he now knew why she'd had that panic attack. Abby was suffering from a type of Post Traumatic Stress Disorder, something he'd become acquainted with after several years of filming in war-torn countries. When he'd started not sleeping, then having flashbacks of the various horrors he'd witnessed, he'd gone to a doctor who'd diagnosed his problem and suggested he go home and do something less stressful. Of course he'd dismissed the doctor's diagnosis as rubbish and kept on filming the world's atrocities till one day a bullet had forced him to come home.

During his recovery he'd read up on PTSD and finally agreed he had been suffering from the condition. Apparently there were only so many rotten things you could see and experience before it affected your well-being. He imagined that for a woman who desperately wanted children even one miscarriage would be distressing. Three definitely qualified as traumatic! Where once Abby had longed to fall pregnant, now just the possibility of falling pregnant set off old hurts which were so full of pain and loss and grief that her whole nervous system had gone berserk.

Unfortunately, Jake didn't think she was in a fit state right now to listen to that kind of logic. What she needed at this moment was kindness and compassion.

'Abby...darling,' he said, holding both her hands tightly as he searched for the right words to say. 'I'm sure Wayne never thought of you as a failure. He obviously loved you very much. And if I know you, I'm sure you were very loving to him in return. As far as your miscarriages are concerned, things like that happen sometimes. One of my sisters-in-law had a couple of miscarriages before she carried a baby full term. There's no reason why this baby—if there is a baby—won't survive, and be born happy and healthy.'

'No, no,' Abby sobbed. 'It won't survive. And I won't be happy. Oh, God, you don't understand.'

'I understand more than you realise. You're crossing your bridges before you come to them, Abby. Why don't we wait and see if you are pregnant? I'll take you to the doctor tomorrow to have a test done. They've made great strides with pregnancy tests these days. They can tell if you are or not even after a few days.'

She snatched her hands away and looked at him then, her expression strangely wary. 'How come you know that?'

'Not for the reason you think. I did a segment on the subject on my show.'

'Oh…'

'And if you are pregnant, then I want you to know that I will stand by you, no matter what you decide to do. I promise I'll be there for you, Abby. Always.'

She stared at him, her eyes still sceptical. Which he supposed was better than sad.

'You won't want to take a pregnant lady overseas with you,' she said.

Jake smiled. 'How do you know?'

'I know.'

'Why don't we just wait and see what the doctor says?'

Abby groaned. 'I really don't want to be pregnant, Jake.'

Not with my baby, Jake thought with some dismay. The temptation to tell her he loved her was acute, but it still didn't feel like the right time.

'Why don't you close your eyes and go to sleep? Then later, when you're feeling better, I'll cook you something for dinner.'

Her chin began to quiver.

'No more tears now,' he said, his voice thick with emotion. 'Everything will be all right, just you wait and see.'

When he returned to the kitchen Sophie was there, looking anxious.

'Did you find out what upset her?'

Jake nodded. 'I'll just get us a drink and then I'll tell you the whole wretched story.'

'Oh, the poor love,' Sophie said once she knew everything. 'No wonder she had a panic attack. So what are you going to do, Jake? I mean, if she *is* pregnant.'

'That rather depends on Abby, don't you think?'

'Would you marry her?'

'In a heartbeat.'

'Did you tell her that?'

'No.'

'Why not?'

'Because I honestly don't think it's what she wants. Not right now.'

'You could be right. There again, you could be wrong.'

Jake rolled his eyes. 'Thanks for the vote of confidence.'

'Sorry. But there are no certainties in life, Jake. Or guarantees. Sometimes you just have to take a risk.'

'That's very good advice,' Jake said thoughtfully, deciding then and there that as soon as the time was right, he would tell Abby that he loved her.

CHAPTER THIRTY

ABBY WAS UNABLE to get an appointment with her doctor until four o'clock the following Friday. Jake had wanted to take her to *his* doctor but Abby had insisted on her own, a very nice female doctor who was both understanding and kind.

In the meantime, Jake had tried to get her to stay at his place but she'd refused, saying she'd prefer to go home after work each day. He'd rung her several times, insisting that he go to the doctor with her. But Abby had refused this as well. She wanted to be alone when she heard the news. She didn't want him to confuse her any more. Bad enough that she was already half wishing that she *was* pregnant. Which was crazy. But it was hard to think straight when you were as deeply in love as she was with Jake.

'Abby Jenkins?' her doctor called out from across the waiting room.

Abby tried to smile as she rose from the chair. But there were no smiles left in her. 'Coming,' she said.

Jake drove into the surgery car park and parked next to Abby's car, having determined to be there for Abby as he'd said he would. He didn't go against her wishes and go inside, but no way was he going to let her leave this appointment without his love and support.

The wait felt interminable. He put some music on to distract his escalating tension, but it didn't work, his stomach doing a somersault when he finally spotted Abby emerging from the building shortly before five.

He was out of his car like a shot, his eyes searching her face for signs of distress as she walked towards him, not finding any comfort in her frown.

'What are you doing here?' she demanded to know straight away. 'I told you not to come.'

'Sorry,' he said straight away. 'I simply had to. So what did the doctor say? Did he do one of the new tests?'

'She's a she and yes, she did a very new test, and no, I'm not pregnant.'

Jake didn't know if he was disappointed or not, though, of course, his main concern was how Abby felt.

'Well, that's good news, isn't it?' he said.

'Yes,' Abby bit out. 'Good news.'

Why, then, he wondered, didn't she *sound* happier?

'I see,' he said, wishing he knew what was going on in her head. 'So what are you going to do now?'

Her sigh was heavy. 'Go home, I suppose.'

'Don't do that. I'd like to take you somewhere for dinner.'

'To celebrate, you mean,' she said with a decided edge in her voice.

'In a way…' Jake thought of the diamond engagement ring he had in his pocket and which he hoped would convince Abby of his feelings for her.

Just then, some more people emerged from the surgery. When a woman started staring at him and pointing, Jake decided it was time for a quick getaway.

'Hop in, Abby,' he said quickly as he reefed open his passenger door. 'Before that woman gets on Twitter and the paparazzi arrive.'

'But what about my car?' she asked even as she did as she was told.

'We'll come back and get it later.' He quickly exited the car park and zoomed up the road.

Abby suddenly bursting into tears brought a groan to his lips, and a swift end to his idea of a romantic dinner. 'Oh, Abby. Darling. Please don't cry. Look, I'll take you home.'

'Yes, please,' she choked out, obviously doing her best to stop crying. But it was no use. The waterworks were open and she kept on weeping.

Jake took her not to her home, but to his. By the time they arrived she'd stopped crying but was looking totally worn out. He parked out front and led her inside, where he offered her either coffee or a glass of wine. She opted for the latter, sliding up on to one of the kitchen stools whilst he did the honours with a bottle of chilled Sauvignon Blanc.

'Can I ask you something, Jake?' she said when he'd poured two generous glasses.

'Of course.'

'What would you have done if the test had come back positive?'

He hesitated, though not for long. 'I was going to ask you to marry me.'

Her silence did not augur well. When Jake

glanced over at her, she was staring at him with shock in her eyes.

'You don't mean that,' she said at last, sounding shaken. 'You don't do marriage and you definitely don't do children. You made that quite clear. You said it was a deal-breaker for you.'

'That was before,' he said.

'Before what?' she demanded, sounding angry now.

'Before I fell in love with you. Actually, I was going to ask you to marry me today, whether you were pregnant or not.'

She shook her head from side to side, her eyes disbelieving.

'But that's crazy, Jake. You're not thinking straight.'

'I had a feeling that might be your reaction,' he said. 'So I thought I had better have backup.'

'A backup?'

'Yep. A backup.'

Jake put down the bottle of wine, his whole body tensing up as he faced a startled Abby, though he tried not to show it.

'Sophie said you were averse to me buying you jewellery but I gather that was because you didn't want me treating you like a mistress. So

I bought the one piece of jewellery which would never be given to a mistress.'

When he brought a small black box out of his pocket and flipped it open, revealing a diamond engagement ring set in yellow gold, Abby stared down at it, then up at him.

'Oh, my God,' she choked out. 'It…it's lovely, Jake. And so are you. I'm touched. Really I am. But I… I can't.'

Dismay made his heart turn over. 'Are you saying that you don't love me?'

The loving look in her eyes was some comfort. 'Of course I love you. Surely you must know that. But I can't marry you. Because marriage means children to me. And I just can't go there again. Not yet. Maybe not ever.'

Jake did his best to hide his hurt and disappointment.

'Can't we just stay as we are, Jake?' she pleaded. 'You know you don't really want marriage, anyway.'

Actually, I don't know any such thing, Jake thought, a great lump filling his throat. After Craig died, he'd realised that his way of life wasn't as great as he'd thought it was. Who wanted to die alone, with no one at their bedside, holding their hand and telling them that they were loved?

Abby's hands clasped the sides of her face, a face full of escalating panic.

'Oh, God, if only you could understand...'

When she looked as if she was about to burst into tears again, Jake knew she was thinking about the babies she had lost. It must have been truly terrible for her. He could see that. He could also see that he had rushed her with his proposal. She wasn't ready to face that kind of commitment.

But one day she would be. And when she was he would be right there by her side.

Slipping the ring box back into his pocket, he smiled over at her. 'It's all right, Abby,' he said gently. 'We'll do what you want and just go on as we are. But could you at least move in with me?'

She lifted adoring eyes to his. 'Oh. Yes. I'd love to.'

CHAPTER THIRTY-ONE

Twelve months later...

'IT WILL BE so good to see Megan and Timmy again,' Abby said excitedly as the plane started its descent into Mascot. 'And your family too.'

'We'll see them all on Christmas Day,' Jake told her. 'I booked the same boat we had last year.'

'Did you? You didn't tell me that.' Which surprised Abby. Because she and Jake told each other everything. During the last year, their love for each other had deepened to a true love. It wasn't just lust, as Abby had once feared. Travelling together, living together, twenty-four-seven had been marvellous. She'd loved every minute of it. Paris in the summer had been magnificent, even if she had picked up a tummy bug. But honestly, she was glad to be home.

'I wanted to surprise you,' Jake went on. 'I have another surprise for you as well.'

'What?'

'Tomorrow morning you have an appointment with one of Sydney's top fertility experts.'

Abby sucked in sharply, her stomach tightening as well. 'You…you shouldn't have done that without talking to me first.'

'Abby,' Jake said gently but firmly, 'it's time.'

And it was. He was right. During the last year, Jake had convinced Abby that he really would like to marry her. And one or two children would be all right by him. And whilst she'd remained on the Pill they had stopped using condoms. But there wasn't a single day that she forgot to take that Pill; she'd programmed her phone with a reminder.

The trouble was, Abby was still afraid. Afraid of hoping and wanting and having her dreams dashed one more time.

'If all else fails,' Jake said, 'we can adopt.'

Her eyes widened. 'Are you sure?'

'Absolutely. There are a lot of wretched orphans in this world who would love a wonderful woman like you as their mother.'

Abby's heart melted with love for this man. 'That's the nicest thing you've ever said to me.'

Jake smiled. 'So when we get home can I drag

out that engagement ring which is still sitting in a drawer somewhere?'

'Oh, God, I still feel awful about that ring. Have you forgiven me for turning down your proposal that day?'

'There's nothing to forgive. You were right to turn me down. It was too soon. But it's not too soon now, Abby. It's time for us to face the future together.'

Jake watched Abby fiddling with her ring as they waited for their turn with the doctor. She was terribly nervous. But then so was Jake. He knew how much having children meant to Abby. He'd seen the look in her eyes every time they'd come across a happy family during their overseas travels. Becoming a father still wasn't an all-consuming dream of his but anything that made Abby happy would make him happy.

The door to the doctor's office opened and Dr Gard walked out. She was about fifty, tall and slim with a plain but kind face.

'Mr and Mrs Sanderson?' she asked, whereupon Abby threw Jake a wry smile.

They traipsed after the doctor into her rooms, where she waved them to two chairs in front of her desk. Clearly, she often saw couples together.

Jake listened to Abby bravely tell her whole medical history, even though her voice was shaking. The doctor listened intently, throwing in a question every now and then.

'I think, Abby,' she said at last, 'that I should examine you. Would you mind?'

Of course she didn't mind and was taken behind a curtain for what felt like an eternity to Jake. Finally, the two women emerged with the doctor's expression a rather puzzled one.

'Well,' she said once they were both seated again, 'I have to confess that this doesn't happen to me very often.'

'What?' Jake asked immediately, sensing that it wasn't all bad news.

Her eyes were directed at Abby. 'You said you were on the Pill?'

'Yes,' Abby replied.

'And you've been having regular periods?'

Abby flushed. 'Well, not exactly. We've been travelling and I've been skipping the white pills so that I didn't have to worry about periods.'

'I see,' the doctor said with a smile. 'Well, Abby, I am happy to inform you that you're actually pregnant.'

'Pregnant!' Abby gasped whilst Jake held his breath. His head was whirling.

'Yes. About four months, by the feel of your uterus. We'll know for sure when you have an ultrasound. I'll organise one for you straight away.'

Both Abby and Jake were in shock as they were taken into another room for the ultrasound. But underneath the shock lay the hope of happiness. If the doctor was right, then Abby was already past the three-month danger time, which was further than she'd ever got before.

Jake held her hand whilst the doctor moved the instrument over Abby's gelled-up stomach, which did indeed have a small baby bump. She'd complained only the other day that she'd put on weight, blaming all the restaurant food they'd been eating. But it hadn't been that. It had been a baby. *His* baby.

Jake's heart turned over as he stared at the screen and saw the outline of a living, breathing human being.

'A little more than four months, I would say,' the doctor told them. 'Do you want to know the sex?'

'Yes, please,' they both chorused.

'It's a girl. Small but beautifully formed.'

'Oh,' Abby said through her tears.

Jake lifted her hand to his lips. 'Just like her mother,' he said, his heart so full of love for this woman, and his child, he was almost in tears himself. He vowed then and there that he would be the best husband and father. Just like his own dad, who he saw now might not have had wealth, but had been rich with love.

'You…you think I'll be all right then?' Abby tentatively asked the doctor.

The woman smiled down at her. 'I'm sure you'll be fine. After all, you have a very good doctor. Don't you worry, dear. I'll look after you.'

EPILOGUE

THE DOCTOR WAS as good as her word. Jake and Abby's daughter went full term. She came into the world a very beautiful baby with a soft crown of fair hair, big blue eyes and the prettiest little face. The birth was a natural one but with enough drugs to make sure Abby wasn't in too much pain.

After the birth, Abby could not stop looking at her daughter, and cuddling her. Jake hardly got a look in. Not that he minded. He knew how much having this baby meant to Abby. Finally, after she'd had her fill, she handed the bundle over for him to hold.

Parental love squeezed Jake's heart as he rocked his daughter to and fro.

'Paris,' he murmured. It was the name they'd chosen once they worked out that that was where she'd been conceived, the doctor explaining that the gastric bug Abby had caught had probably rendered the Pill ineffective for a few days.

'Well, Mrs Sanderson,' he said with the fatuous smile of a besotted father, 'you've produced a real beauty here.'

'She is lovely, isn't she?'

'She's the spitting image of her mother.'

'Do you think so?'

He did, and so did everyone else who came in to visit them. Sometimes, there were so many people in Abby's room that the nurses would complain about the noise. The maternity ward breathed a sigh of relief when Jake took Abby and Paris home.

Sophie and Megan were asked to be godparents at the baby's christening three weeks later, both of them receiving very generous gifts from the happy parents. Abby gave an over-the-moon Megan her old house and Jake presented Sophie with the deed to Craig's apartment.

The following Christmas was an especially joyful one. Jake hired the same boat for another harbour cruise, amazed at how much he enjoyed the family gathering, perhaps because he could show off his very beautiful daughter. Abby revelled in everyone's compliments plus the knowledge that, at last, her dream of creating her own happy family had finally come true. Already she was planning a second baby, and Jake was happy to oblige. Truly, for a man who'd once claimed not to want marriage and children, he'd proved to be a wonderful husband and father.

'She was a big hit, wasn't she?' Jake said that night as they stood next to Paris's pretty pink cot and stared down at her sleeping form.

When he slipped a tender arm around Abby's waist, she leant her head against his and sighed. 'It was a wonderful Christmas Day. Even better than last year.'

Jake had to agree. Though last year's Christmas had been pretty special. It had been, after all, their wedding day as well. Which reminded him.

'I have a surprise present for you,' he said. And he produced another ring box, which contained an emerald and diamond eternity ring.

'Oh, Jake,' Abby choked out as he slipped it on her finger. 'It's beautiful.'

'Not as beautiful as you, my darling.'

'You say the loveliest things to me.'

'That's because I love you.'

'I'm still not sure why, but I'm glad that you do.'

Jake bent his head and kissed her. He could think of a thousand reasons why he loved Abby, not the least that she was the bravest, kindest, most genuine person he'd ever met. He thanked his uncle every day for the legacy which had set him on a path that showed him marriage and children need not be a grind; they could be a joy. He'd never been happier than during the last year. Of course, he was lucky that he didn't have to work if he didn't want to. But Jake knew he would not enjoy being idle for long. He was already thinking of creating a series of documentaries called the *Honeymoon Show*, highlighting places to go for a honeymoon, a feel-good show full of happy people who actually loved each other.

Now that would be different…

When Abby gave a small moan of desire, his head lifted.

'Time for bed, I think, my love.' And, taking Abby's hand in his, he walked off with her into the future.

* * * * *